STORIES OF THE EYE

EDITED BY
SAM RICHARD
& JOE KOCH

CONTENTS

THE EYE INVERTED

THE EDITORS

The ways we make, remake, and unmake one another through looking, touching, and action; the changes wrought in an observer by the impossible task of claiming no measurable effect upon their subject; the creative urge that molds the creator into a new shape as much as they seem to mold their art: such musings about our interconnectedness and complicity as makers of art had long troubled us when we came up with the idea for Stories of the Eye.

In the process of making art, we change. By art, we mean any number of creative endeavors showcased here including painting, dancing, sewing, sketching, mimicking, trapping, preserving, and the invoking of abyssal gods, to name a few. Understanding the mechanism of change and considering what boundaries we hold around controlling change during the creation of art seems like one key to unlocking the process. (Yes, we like turning things inside out.) And although the original concept was intended to inspire stories oriented more towards relationship and communicative interactions, I think our collective survival through Covid's initial wave of pandemic isolation burned away some of the threads linking us with the outside and resulted in authors telling stories more centered on the inside. The "eye" inverted.

It feels right at this time in history to lean into these more introspective journeys. What better place to find change? Transcendence, even?

THE ANEURYTIC

ANDREW WILMOT

"Thou shalt not be an unoriginal twat."

— LEVITICUS, 27:35

I.

WHEN HANS FIRST MET THE "ANEURYTIC" ARTIST, HE HAD LONG GONE BY the name Leviticus. He'd seemed so proud of his moniker, as if it had taken him years of quiet rumination and wasn't just some guttural invective looted from a first year's artist's manifesto.

Now, standing atop a roiling mountain range of disembowelled books and canvases pulled from their frames, of clay and stone and marble sculptures smashed to confetti, Leviticus spoke only of hypocrisy. Hans watched from the rear of the crowd as battle-scarred painters, sculptors, photographers, and writers alike cheered their savior on, their hands clutching packets of matches and lighters and liquor bottles stuffed with oil-soaked rags.

Beneath his coat, Hans felt the weight of his sketchbook growing heavier, growing hot. As Molotov cocktails were lit to both sides of him, he saw the keloid-white cross-hatching on the faces and arms of those who'd followed Leviticus to this vanishing point, from which there was no return.

Their unexpected champion extended his arms in invitation. The congregation responded by hurling their makeshift explosives toward the misshapen pyramid of creation at Leviticus' feet. Hans ducked down beneath rows of outstretched arms drawing flaming arcs across the dark winter sky, and disappeared out the far end of the farmer's field on which they'd lit their history aflame.

II.

His real name was Levine.

"What's your last name?" Hans asked as they spooned on the couch in Hans' studio.

"I don't have one."

"You don't have any parents?"

Leviticus paused. "I killed a man," he said suddenly, flatly. "He wanted to destroy the world, so I killed him and cut free my name. Severed it like an artery from which my past bled out and died."

Hans frowned. "You have a past. You might think you've gotten rid of it, but it's still there." He hesitated. "You didn't actually kill a man, did you?"

"I told you, he was trying to destroy the world."

"How?"

"By being uninteresting."

III.

Hans first heard of Leviticus while in fourth year. He'd arrived on campus to find the Dean and the university's security force surrounding a Rembrandt that had at one point been housed in the seventh-floor library archives but now hung suspended from the ceiling of the convocation mall by heavy fisherman's rope. The painting itself had been desecrated; several wide lacerations marked the canvas with an alphanumeric signature, "L:27:35."

"What's the 'L' stand for?" said a student to Hans' left. "Leviticus?"

"Can't be," said another. "There's no 27:35 in Leviticus."

"It's him," a third said excitedly. Hans turned, recognizing Clara's voice; they were in the same year.

"Who's 'him'?" he asked.

Clara scrunched up her face with the same discourteous look she gave during studio crits. "The Annihilator," she said. "Leviticus. He's here." When Hans didn't immediately respond, she audibly scoffed. She said Leviticus fashioned himself "a better Banksy," but instead of interventions, the man she called The Annihilator and "the Eraser" was provoked conceptually by elimination. "No one knows who he really is."

"What do you mean by 'elimination'?"

"He wants to burn everything down and start fresh. Better watch yourself, Hans. He'll probably start with you."

"What's that supposed to mean?"

"He's only interested in originality," She spun and started off. "You don't have a chance."

IV.

Hans was the last to leave the studio that night, as was often the case. While busily using a metal dog grooming comb to expel gelatinous clumps of oil paint from a two-inch brush, he heard a loud crash and the clang of several metal instruments falling to the ground.

He slowly craned his head around a short wall and peered into the exhibition space. On the ground was an open brown leather satchel and several paint-stained kitchen knives, X-Acto blades, and BIC lighters.

"Shit."

Hans looked up. Partially hidden in the rafters of the converted textile factory-cum-artists' studio was a man in his early thirties looping a length of rope around one of the horizontal beams. Suspended from the rope was a large four-by-four canvas painting. The oils were not yet dry; the rope stroked ribbed fault lines across its surface like a child making an angel in the snow.

"What are you doing to my work!" Hans cried.

"Destroying it," answered the man. "Like you should've done the moment you finished."

Hans picked one of the knives up off the ground and jogged over to his painting. Started sawing through the taught rope.

"Stop! Leave that alone."

Hans grunted as he proceeded to cut through the thick, fibrous cord. "I'm going to salvage what I can and then I'm going to report your ass to the police. Breaking and entering, destruction of property—"

"You can't do that."

"The fuck I can't."

The man scrabbled across the rafters to a ladder propped against the wall. He climbed down quickly, dropping the final few rungs to the ground. Hans placed the canvas gently on the studio floor, freeing the last of the paint-coated rope from its damaged face.

Hans straightened up and thrust the knife out in front of him as the man approached. "Not another step." His arm was shaking. "I'll use this."

"No you won't."

"You're him, aren't you? The one who cut up the Rembrandt? Leviticus."

The man bowed. "At your service."

"Shut up!" Hans flicked his eyes down. "You ruined it. You... you shit!"

Leviticus smiled with satisfaction. "That was sort of the point." He nodded to the canvas. Visible between the waves created by the rope was a detailed black and white portrait of a family of four—Hans included—sitting together on a couch, nude. "This is your family, right? *Why* are they naked?"

"First you deface it, now you want to know why I painted it?"

"Enlighten me. Give me your rationale, and I'll give you mine."

"Quid pro fuck you."

"I'm interested. Truly."

A sudden pang of heartache gripped Hans' insides. "I wanted

to show them in a different light—my parents and sister. It's about vulnerability and—"

"It's shit," said Leviticus. "Unmitigated, unoriginal *shit.*"

"What?"

"You think you're the first artist to fetishize their family?" He dismissed Hans with a wave of his hand. "You aren't even the first in your class."

"What's your problem?"

"There's still hope for you. You're unoriginal but not entirely without talent." Leviticus backed away, glancing over his shoulder to the open window through which he'd entered.

"Don't you dare," said Hans.

"You're not going to hurt me, and you're not going to turn me in." Leviticus pivoted and darted for the window. He swung one leg over the ledge and hesitated. Looked back. Hans was fixed in place. Leviticus reached into his pocket and removed a plastic baggie containing a flat pink pill the size of a fingernail and placed it on the windowsill.

"For you," he said, and pulled himself out the window. "Be the artist you should have been."

V.

Hans hadn't thought anything of the pill—not at first. He left the studio that night with it tucked inside the satchel of Leviticus' tools, determined first thing in the morning to call the police and file a report.

Before any of that, however, he went home and started researching his unexpected nemesis online. What he found was more of what he'd already seen: tales of an elusive vandal defacing and in some cases outright destroying famous and not-so-famous works of art with equal degrees of condemnation. Most called him a criminal, a renegade artist with a chip on his shoulder; others seemed inexplicably in awe of Leviticus' apparent crusade to rid the world of works of mediocrity; of art he deemed unworthy.

The earliest accounts had him setting fire to work stolen from independent studios. Eventually he moved on from fire to blades, and was identified walking into privately owned galleries and public collections dressed all in black, weapons stuffed up his sleeves. It wasn't until a year into his "crusade" that his alphanumeric signature first appeared, viciously opening the face of Pollock's *One: Number 31, 1950*, on display at the MoMA.

Nothing, however, about a little pink pill.

Hans was intrigued, but not convinced, by the unspoken rationale by which Leviticus operated. Much of what had so far been destroyed were famous works of art, or pieces with direct antecedents—portraiture and pastorals, iconography and religious works directly or indirectly inspired by artists who'd come before.

The following morning, as Clara examined Hans' scarred painting, he asked what she knew about Leviticus.

"He was here, wasn't he?" she said excitedly. "He did this to your painting?"

"Don't sound so thrilled."

"He did you a favor. *Trust me.*"

"Can you not right now?"

"You know what your problem is, Hans?"

"I really don't ca—"

"You think you're good." She sneered at his wounded canvas. "You're under the impression that shit like this is original. Risk-taking. It's *not*."

"And destroying the works of others is original *how*?"

"You don't get it. You're just so...prosaic."

She walked away then. Hans watched, saw her reach into her pocket and pull out something small, something pink, which she quickly popped into her mouth.

VI.

Hans and Leviticus crossed paths again a year later. Hans was renting a small studio space on the fourth floor of a turn-of-the-century building that had been home to no fewer than five newspapers. The smell of ink and unfiltered cigarettes was imbedded thick in every square inch of pockmarked brick and concrete. When he found the padlock open at his feet, he naturally feared the worst.

Leviticus stood with his back to the door, a large, half-finished canvas at his knees, in his hand a gleaming chef's knife. The brown leather satchel he'd left behind that night was open, resting on the short, paint-spackled table by the window.

"Your talent is wasted on pretty pictures and portraiture."

"What do you want?"

Leviticus nodded at the open satchel of knives. "You had something of mine. I came to get it back."

"Then take them and go."

Leviticus' shoulders slumped. He placed the chef's knife in the satchel and tucked it under his arm. Hans backed away as Leviticus made for the exit. The Annihilator paused in the doorway, turned back around.

"Why did you hold onto this?" He held the satchel high. "You could have turned it over to the authorities." He paused. "You took it, didn't you? The gift I left for you that night."

"You mean this?" Hans withdrew the pink pill, still in its plastic baggie, from the pocket of his jeans.

"But you've kept it on your person all this time." Paused. "You know what it does. You've *seen* it."

"After that night, yeah, I started seeing this little pink disaster all over the place—tucked away in tool kits, crushed up and snorted off light tables. People in my class...they started to change. Their work devolved into *nothingness*. Meaningless abstraction. They all whispered about you at first, like it was some big secret. Started invoking your name in studio crits as if you were the second coming. I bet not one of them knows who you really are."

"Tell me—who am I?"

Hans stuffed the pill back into his pocket. "Point blank? You're a grifter and a small-time drug peddler who gets off slicing up other people's art and thinking that somehow makes it yours."

"Is that all?"

"Bit of a prick, too."

Leviticus grinned.

"What is it? The pill—what does it do?"

"It's an aneurytic."

"A what?"

"It creates micro-hemorrhages of a non-lethal variety. Designed to target the memory and image centers of the brain and offer a temporary tabula rasa—to give an artist space and time to think for themselves, without the burden of history."

Hans' mouth was agape. "Micro-hemorrhages . . ."

"*Non-lethal* hemorrhages, yes."

"You're insane. Why? What's the point of all this?"

Leviticus closed the distance between them; came close enough that Hans could feel the heat of his breath.

"Because we are *mendacious*," Leviticus said. "There's no such thing as creativity anymore. Just piety. Reverence and mimicry." He pointed to a stack of portraits leaning against the studio wall. "Today's art is devotional shit masturbating to the art of yesterday, of hundreds of years gone by. Only way to move forward is to strip it all away."

He leaned forward suddenly and kissed Hans tenderly on the forehead. Reached down and gently patted the pocket containing the aneurytic.

"It's all right if you're not ready to see what I see," Leviticus said. "Take the pill and go to work. You'll understand then."

"I won't," Hans croaked.

Leviticus backed into the doorway. "But you won't turn me in, either." He paused. "Maybe you just need a push in the right direction."

Hans instinctively moved between Leviticus and the stack of canvases.

Leviticus laughed, turned away. "Be seeing you," he called over his shoulder before vanishing from sight, leaving Hans alone in his studio.

VII.

"Heard he was a chemist in a previous life."

Hans watched as Janelle swayed on her feet. The half-empty champagne glass in her right hand tipped precipitously toward the gallery's floor.

"You've tried it then?" Janelle nodded drunkenly. "What's it like?"

"It's like...there's this pop inside your head, and you start feeling fuzzy, like your brain's carbonated. You don't even notice... you don't know what you *should* be doing, you just know you need to do *something*." She paused. "It's...It's freedom."

This "freedom" was on full display that night. Hans had run into Janelle, whom he hadn't seen since graduation, upon arriving at the Wallace Satellite for the opening of a new group exhibit titled *Open Vein*. He hadn't known any of the artists named in the exhibition. But seeing Janelle there, and noting the new and all-too-visible cross-hatching of scar tissue on her face and neck, he realized whose world he'd stepped into.

The art on the walls was abstracted to an extreme, with canvases of all sizes that looked as if they'd been painted using toilet brushes, construction tools, and steel wool. Every one of them: *Untitled*. However, the art was only half of Hans' discomfort; every artist there, and indeed many of the patrons, were scarred or burned on their faces and limbs. Some wounds looked old and had healed into pale surface arteries, while others appeared red and frayed and decidedly...fresh.

Janelle caught his eyes lingering on the scar tissue on her cheek. "Beautiful, isn't it?"

He glanced at the other razor-slashed faces in the crowd, quickly digesting his revulsion. "I don't think I understand."

"There's nothing *to* understand." She produced an aneurytic and placed it on her tongue. Pulled Hans forward and kissed him, passing the pill between them before pushing him away. "It's about unmaking yourself."

Hans ran outside and spat the mostly dissolved pill into the street. It was too late, though; he felt the slight fizz of his world slipping away, losing shape, losing color. In his panic he tripped and fell, face-planting into the sidewalk.

When he raised his head off the pavement, the world around him was unfamiliar: a thinly drawn skeleton without context.

VIII.

Hans arrived at his studio the next morning, tired and ingloriously hung over.

Inside, Leviticus sat cross-legged at one end of the knotty forest-green sofa set against the far wall. "What kind of name is Hans Saito anyway?" he asked as Hans entered and shut the door behind him.

Hans sighed. "My mother was a German ex-pat living in Tokyo, where she met my father."

Leviticus squinted. "Not much of mom in you, is there?"

Hans draped his coat over the far end of the sofa and folded his arms. "What the hell kind of name is Leviticus?"

"It's the name I chose for myself. Represents—"

"Rhetorical question. Don't care." Leviticus huffed. "It isn't *real*. It's just something you've adopted—like the rest of this whole bullshit forget-me-please art movement."

"It's not just about art."

Hans waved dismissively. "Either put your name to it or I'm calling shenanigans on this whole thing."

"What's in a name, Hans?"

"*Integrity*. Says you're willing to stand for your ideas."

"Oh please. Your name says absolutely nothing about anything except that you are, for whatever reason, beholden to your past."

"What *is it* about you and the past?"

Leviticus' face reddened. "Don't you ever think to yourself, we're all just stuck in place? When people say, 'This person's the new Shakespeare, or Michelangelo, or da Vinci,' what they're really saying is that our past is inescapable. It's a millstone around our necks—a hindrance to true creativity."

"That's your whole thing, isn't it? To free us from this hindrance?"

Leviticus straightened up. "I'm your very own swarm of locusts, drying rivers, and withering cattle."

"You do love to hear yourself talk. You've already got your knives back, why are you here?"

Leviticus sat back down. Made himself comfortable. "I saw you last night. At the opening."

"You were there?"

Leviticus nodded. "No one but you knows what I look like."

"I don't see any scars on you—you'd have stuck out like a sore thumb."

He held up his hands, palms out. The skin of each was red and mangled, with wide ridges resembling mountain ranges as seen from space. It looked as if the flesh of his hands had been burned and sliced open before being glued back together again.

Hans recoiled. Leviticus dropped his palms to his knees. "I saw that girl kissing you. I know what she did. Tell me...what did you see?"

"You don't know?"

"No two brains are alike, so no two reactions are ever the same."

"Well now I feel safe."

Leviticus fixed Hans with a shit-eating grin. "Safety has no place in art."

Hans hesitated. "It was quicker than I expected. Seconds at best. It was like...all color was siphoned out of the world, leaving only an outline."

Leviticus leaned forward eagerly. "What else?"

"Nothing. I vomited up what I could and slept it off."

Leviticus stood abruptly and stalked to the door. "I was wrong about you," he said, guarding his arms as if Han's words were razors across his wrists. "You're not ready."

"Not ready for what? You stormed into *my* life, remember?"

Leviticus shook his head. "You're still a child. It was wrong of me to come back here." He left without looking back.

IX.

Time passed, and small artist-run centers and local indie galleries expressed moderate interest in Hans' portraits and their "classical" approach. He was taken aback at first, but another type of work had squeezed out all competition. Larger gallery owners rushed to applaud the inventiveness of these new creators and their choice to represent, really, nothing at all. Soon the work of aneurytic artists became the norm they'd sought to undermine; complacency in their total rejection of form.

The shootings began the same night three artists, half a world away, clad in facial lacerations so deep as to mask their identities, stole into the Galleria dell'Accademia di Firenze and took twenty-pound sledgehammers to Michelangelo's *David*.

The first shooting was reported by a man out walking his dog in the industrial district: he was passing a small studio on the ground floor of an old office building when he heard a loud *crack*, followed by screaming. The man followed the racket to a window and saw a wiry, anaemic-looking young man holding a gun in one hand as his other hovered shakily in front of a blood-splattered sheet of plywood painted picket-fence white.

The response from the community was prompt and aggressive. Within two weeks, *Open Vein 2* was announced—an all-wounds exhibition. Most of the artists involved missed the opening night gala due to an overwhelming number of hospitalizations. Those who made it sported bloodied, gauze-wrapped limbs with filthy bandages days unchanged, borne like martyr's wounds.

All were trumped, however, by the exhibition's crown jewel—a stark white canvas, eight feet tall and three feet wide, with a red thousand-point star at its centre. It lay thick, with grey and white chunks throughout like globules of paint trapped in place, lacquered over with a fast-drying agent.

The wife of the artist stood stoic by the canvas, dressed in funeral black, from shoes to floppy southern belle sunhat. She clutched a single red rose in her black-gloved hands. To the other side, the artist's statement—his suicide note. The wife was arrested before the night was over, having been the one who pulled the trigger. The ensuing conversation paid little attention to legalities and focused instead on the actual identity of the artist: the husband who'd conceived the piece, or his wife who had executed it. And him.

It was on the exhibition's final night that Leviticus finally revealed himself. He urged his public on, convincing them to press forward by destroying that which they themselves had produced, to never allow their art to repeat—to never become a mockery of itself or, worse, inspiration to another.

Hans was there, among the injured but invigorated crowd. As Leviticus spoke, people to Hans' left and right passed around large plastic bags filled with aneurytics. One by one they wiped themselves of what they'd just witnessed, of all inspiration, all influence, all possibility of creative intervention.

For the first time, Hans felt as if he were seeing the man behind the moniker. He watched as Leviticus jubilantly passed through the crowd, always with a pill on his tongue, which he gifted freely to every person he kissed. He stopped suddenly, face to face with Hans.

The two men stared at one another for several seconds, the air between them pregnant with mistrust. Hans, shaking, opened his mouth to receive.

Leviticus simply moved on, to the woman to Hans' left, continuing until all but Hans had been saved.

X.

The stories continued:

He was a chemist who'd experimented on himself to unlock his "creative potential."

He was an arsonist who'd given rationale to his incendiary "work."

He was a vicious art collector hell bent on eliminating all competition.

These possibilities and more cycled through Hans' mind when Leviticus again appeared in his studio. This time, however,

Leviticus was framed by empty space; the only items left were an easel heavy and spackled with paint, the table, and the couch.

"You've thrown it all away," said Leviticus.

"Moved them to a safer place. I didn't trust the neighborhood."

"If you'd only trusted yourself and gotten rid of them we wouldn't be having this conversation."

"I know how to rectify that." Hans held open the studio door.

"You don't really want me to go."

"You're always telling me what I want or don't want. I'm done. I'm sick of it."

Leviticus stood before him, arms at his sides, palms outward. "My name is Levine."

Hans sighed. "Why are you telling me this?"

Levine crossed the distance between them. Cupped the back of Hans' head and drew him in for a kiss. Hans allowed it, but only briefly. He turned away. Felt Levine's breath on his neck, damp like late July. Levine pulled Hans toward the couch. Slipped off his shirt, then Hans' shirt, and tossed both to the ground; pulled from his pocket a single pink aneurytic and placed it on the tip of his tongue. Unsure, Hans slowly lowered himself on top of Levine's weathered body, and linked their lips and tongue together.

XI.

Hans' head felt wrapped in fiberglass insulation. Levine lay asleep next to him on the couch. Instinctively, Hans reached for a small, leather sketchbook that had been tucked beneath the tools on the table. He opened to a blank page and stared at Leviticus—Levine —lost in a deep sleep. He simply looked like a man. Barely more than a boy in many respects. Certainly not the figurehead he'd transformed into, either by design or through circumstance.

Hans started to sketch.

Levine woke an hour later. He saw Hans sitting across from him and smiled sweetly. It was only when he'd fully opened his eyes that he saw the graphite in Hans' hand.

"What are you doing?"

"You looked peaceful," Hans said without looking up. "I wanted to remember it."

"Then come over here and start remembering."

"I'm almost done."

"No, really—put the book *down*."

Hans continued drawing.

Levine rolled off the couch and grabbed for the sketchbook. Hans clutched it to his chest. Levine snatched at it a second time and Hans scrabbled up and backed against the wall.

"What's gotten into you?" Hans demanded.

Instead of answering, Leviticus gathered his things; slipped on his pants and fumbled with his belt. In the soft morning light, Hans could see every burn mark and abrasion adorning his lithe, wintery body—tattooed memories of past crimes.

"I thought we shared something last night," Levine said. "You tasted it; I know you did."

"It-it didn't work."

"Liar!"

"I'm telling the truth! Things changed at first, but...It didn't last, Levine."

"*Don't* call me that!"

"I...I just wanted to capture the moment."

"Moments aren't for capturing, *Hans Saito*. They're meant to pass." He quieted. "Nothing you do is original."

"And you're the paragon of that?" Hans, incensed, stepped away from the wall.

"I am—"

"A swarm of locusts and withering cattle. Yeah, I got it. But so is everyone else. You've got people around the world taking your shitty little pills and pushing this cult of 'the now,' and you know what? Everyone's so goddamn original that no one is. All your precious little snowflakes are starting to bleed the same blood and for *what*? To be the very thing you wanted to kneecap in the first place? *Fuck you*—I'll make what I want, thank you very much."

Levine stood silent in the face of Hans' outburst. Unmoved. Then stormed out, shirt balled in his fist.

Alone again, Hans slumped back against the wall and slid to the ground.

XII.

Hans stopped at the Wallace Satellite the next morning. He peered inside the large front window. The lights were off and all artwork had been stripped from the walls. It was the same at the Contemporary Art Gallery down the street, and the Patterson-Morris Collection two blocks farther.

As he stared, an emaciated figure sidled up beside him. He glanced to his right to find Janelle looking as much a zombie as he felt. The cross-hatching on her neck now travelled all the way down her shoulder and arm, ending at her wrist.

"It's done," she said. "Last night everyone stormed in and tore their work from the walls. They tossed it all into the back of a flatbed pickup. *He* asked them to do it, they said. Said it was the next step."

"What next step?" Hans asked.

Janelle handed Hans a scrap of paper torn from the edge of an arterial collage he recognized from *Open Vein 2*. Sketched hastily through the artfully drawn blood splotches was a map leading just outside of town.

"They're going to burn it. When the sun goes down. They're going to burn everything."

XIII.

Hans made his way to the spot marked on the map—a farmer's field south of the city, off Route 401—and parked at the end of a long row of vehicles stretching all the way around the plot. He heard the commotion as soon as he opened the door.

The field was cluttered and cacophonous, with burned, scarred, and otherwise wounded artists dotting the tall, dry winter grass like ants on a hill. In the centre of it all, standing atop a winding mountain of broken, torn, and half-destroyed works of art, Leviticus preached to his followers.

"In our sacrifice we cast off the shackles of our past and are reborn!"

Hans watched, frightened and all too aware of the weight of the sketchbook he clutched to his chest, hidden from all, as Leviticus danced atop the bones of his own movement; as the flock set fire to the pieces of their selves, smashed and shattered, piled at his feet.

Hans remained at the rear of the crowd, ducking as Molotov cocktails were hurled overhead. He held himself tight, afraid that at any minute one of Leviticus' followers would somehow, amidst the popping and fizzing of their degrading memories, recognize him and drag him before their leader.

Eventually, the noise stopped. In its place, a stark, unsettling silence descended. Hans felt a growing arrhythmia like thunder in his eardrums. He stared ahead just in time to see the fire rising, enveloping Leviticus where he stood, arms upraised. Encased in flames, the aneurytic artist fell to his knees and thrashed around on top of the burning pile, crashing down its side to land at the feet of his flock. They backed away instinctively, to protect themselves. Stood there immobile, unsure if this had been his endgame all along. A few looked as if they wanted to strip their shirts and douse the flames. They didn't.

As Leviticus' thrashing slowed and then ceased altogether, many of his followers paused to take in what had just transpired. And as the flames quieted, and fell, they turned and walked in communal silence across the dead, brown grass, away from the devastation. Unable, or unwilling, to look at one another.

Hans observed from his car as the last of Leviticus' followers departed, leaving behind the charred, ashen remains of their work and the shriveled corpse of a man whose real name was Levine. A man who no longer looked anything like the man in the pages of Hans' sketchbook.

THE THING THAT MOVES THE MEAT

M. LOPES DA SILVA

They like me, but they do not love me. They can't love me; they are in love with the invisible thing that moves my meat.

They explained it to me when I met them. "I'm painting the spiritual limbic. The arcane liquidity that we only bear witness to in actions."

"What?" I asked them. They wore a single playing card torn in half as earrings – the jack of clubs split down the middle. Their sidecut's fade was so clean I wanted to run my index finger down its incline into the soft divot behind their ear.

"The invisible thing that moves your meat," they said.

"My soul?"

They shrugged. "Whatever you'd like to call it."

"You're trying to paint souls?"

They frowned. "I'm trying to decipher the anatomy of the unseen."

"Okay," I said. "What does my soul look like?"

"Never mind," they said. "This isn't going to work."

"What? Wait, what did I say?"

"You're too impatient."

"I'm not," I said. "I'm sorry if I said something that bothered you, but I promise that I can be very patient. I've sat for a lot of artists."

They looked at me, their eyes serious and steady, then said. "Get up and move around."

I stood up from the stool in the empty college classroom. It was late, that indigo hour where the lights on the campus buzzed on in orange and the crowds had thinned to clusters of night classes that you could hear, muffled and remote through the walls.

"How should I move?" I asked them.

"How should I know? Just move."

I decided to treat it like modeling for gesture sketches, and started snapping into different poses, only a little faster than usual. I arched my back. I knelt. I bowed. I pointed at a window. I clasped both of my hands around my neck.

"Yes," they said. "That's it! That's fine. Oh god, yes – beautiful!"

And I tried not to let their words matter but each one landed in me like a spark; I was soon warm with the heat of their casual compliments. Something I had not felt in years. They were looking at me. Really looking. Really seeing me.

I tried to remind myself that this feeling wasn't real, just a skittering thing across the brain. A release of chemicals into my bloodstream; an accelerated heart rate; a sudden stutter in my respiratory function.

And then they weren't looking anymore. I felt the absence of their gaze upon my flesh before I saw it; an abrupt chill puckering my exposed skin.

"That will do," they said. "The position's yours if you want it, but I can't pay you much."

I laughed. "You're an artist. Of course you can't pay me much."

Their face reddened, the tendons on the back of their hands went stark; I'd found a raw nerve. "I'll be able to pay you more once my vision gets more traction—"

"I just wanted to work with you," I said.

"Really?" they said. And I felt it again, first as heat then seen: their looking.

"Yes," I said. They kept looking. Their warmth burned me.

But then they stopped looking. It was late. The interview was over. I had to go home. I hurried and got on the train, sliding over the streets of Santa Monica like a cartoon snake, the X-rayed mouse of myself looking out a window. Lost even though I knew the way home.

MY STUDIO APARTMENT is off the books because it's actually a one-car garage that the obscenely wealthy building owner converted into a studio after viewing too many tiny home shows. The bathroom is the afterthought of an afterthought. The night the artist hired me I stared at the sink as I brushed my teeth. I kept the bathroom mirror in my peripheral vision; I model for artists but I don't like looking at myself. A lot of my exes think that's funny, but I don't. I spat toothpaste at the rusty drain, rinsing the glob away with equally rusty water.

It was needing to be looked at that was the problem – that desire, gnawing and demeaning. The modeling work usually fed that. I was accustomed to being observed, really; didn't people look at me every day?

But they didn't. That was the thing. Even when you stood in front of someone naked to the skin and shaking from the cold they could look and only see the vaguest hint of what was really there. A faint outline distorted with their own style and intention. Most people only saw what they were looking for: it was almost impossible for them to witness what was really in front of them at any given time, unless –

I washed my mouth out with water from the tap. Spat it out. A chill from the poured concrete of the floor knived up my legs.

Only the curious really saw things. Or those who cared enough to look. I wanted the latter to be true; I wanted them to care so badly. That was the other thing. Was my desire lying to me? Telling me something I only wanted to think? My thumb twitched over glass. On the surface of my phone they were there: everything about them. The white Latinx non-binary 30-something artist taking the art world by the throat. Their blue eyes and disheveled sidecut and freckle-dotted skin. The critical acclaim of their Out of Tune touring show of several spirit radios that they placed in different rooms of supposedly haunted houses around Los Angeles. The success of their Living Tarot show before that—with hired actors representing the cards of the tarot deck randomly appearing to individual spectators in peepshow rooms at the insertion of a dollar in a slot.

I know too much about them. I already knew too much about them before I showed up for the interview. But my knowledge does nothing to comfort me. It's just an assortment of facts that brings me no closer to them than this job will.

THEY'VE DECIDED to draw me at their studio, a small empty room that the college lets them use. I was unclear about the details of the arrangement that they have with the school, and didn't press them about it. I arrived early, hoping to talk to them. Too early—they weren't there yet. I took out my phone and unintentionally accessed my camera. The camera was reversed, showing me a picture of my face, horrified and stabbing at the screen to turn the damn thing off.

In the middle of all that, they showed up.

They stared, and I flushed with embarrassment but not the heat of their gaze and that's when I realized that they were staring in my direction, but they weren't staring at me. Their brow furrowed as I stabbed the phone. Their fingers kept reaching for their pencil case then hesitating. I put the phone away, and their hand relaxed.

"Hello," I said.

"Yes," they said, nodding at me. "Are you ready?" They withdrew a key from their pocket to open the door. The classroom had desks pushed up against a far wall and little else inside of it.

"Of course," I said, even though I wasn't.

DISROBING WAS UNEVENTFUL – they rummaged around in their pencil case and arranged sketchbooks while I stripped to my underwear. When they appeared to be done, I walked to the center of the room and started moving randomly like I had before.

And then they drew me.

But no, that's not accurate. They didn't draw me at all. They weren't even looking at me; I couldn't feel any warmth from their gaze touching me. When I was able to peek at them, I confirmed it – they were looking right through me. Peering intently at something just above or beyond me. Fascinated with my spiritual limbic.

"What are you doing? Keep moving," they said.

I kept moving. I knelt. I covered my eyes. I touched my toes. It became a kind of dance, odd and without rhythm. Their hand constantly moved across the pages of their sketchbook. There was an instinctual quality to their gesture, reminiscent of automatic writing or the motions of sleepwalkers. Their dance, different but in disjointed time with my own. There was an intimacy to this matched biology, a primal duality, but then I remembered the invisible subject in the room, the one that they were drawing, and I could only feel cold. I was shivering, my shivers moving their pencil across the page until they stopped and tore the page free, crumpled it in their fist.

"Are you cold? You're not moving much. Take a break," they said.

And that flicker of care, quick across me, made me jump with its heat. I stood in front of them, absolutely confused, as they stretched and took a sip of water from a bottle they'd brought with them. I put my robe on, and headed towards their sketches, intent on taking a look for myself.

"Oh no, not yet. This is going to take a while. I'll show you the finished pieces, I promise. But not these," they said.

"Oh, okay," I said. But it wasn't. Not a bit.

THAT NIGHT I went home to yet another message on my phone from my mother misgendering me. The only person I had come out to, and she never bothered to get it right. It was difficult to imagine anyone bothering to get it right. Anyone seeing me completely. There were moments of recognition, slim like waning moons, but they seemed too few and far between. Most days were overcast with bullshit like this one.

I deleted the phone message and tried to look at profiles on the dating app I'd downloaded. People were interested in me, or more accurately interested in the pictures that I'd chosen to post, because I barely dared to put anything about myself up there. My 33 years of age were there. My interest in art museums. I used to have my career posted, but too many bizarro inquiries get sent to an "artist's model." I tried to focus on the multitudes of faces on my phone screen, but they were the one I wanted to look at. I gave up and put the phone away.

"KEEP MOVING," they said.

"I'm tired," I said. I wasn't tired, but I still said it.

Frustrated, they put their charcoal stick aside. "Fine, take a break."

"Why don't you draw me instead? Just for fun. It'll make it easier on me."

They frowned. "Take your break," they said. They got up and collected their sketches together. Took a sip from their ever-ready water bottle.

I put my robe on. Went up to them. "Any finished sketches today?"

"Not yet."

"That's a shame. I'd really like to see them."

They scrubbed the shaved part of their head with their stained fingers, smearing charcoal into their stubble. "It's not happening any time soon," they said.

"Well, can you at least tell me what my soul looks like?"

More charcoal darkened their stubble. "Like energy. Like raw forceful *power*."

That shocked me. "Really?"

"I don't lie about the spiritual limbic."

"Does it look like electricity?"

"No."

"What does it look like?" I asked. But they just sat down and frowned at me. Took out a ballpoint pen and started chewing on the end of it.

Finally, when the pause had gone so long I'd half-forgotten what I asked, they said: "It looks like something inside of myself."

"What do you mean?" I said, but they wouldn't answer me.

THEY CAN'T LOVE ME. It's impossible for them to love me. How can they love this jumbled assortment of sacrospinal ligament, acromion, and gastrocnemius? This absolute chaos of blood vessels and bacteria? This disgusting pile of living, dying, breathing meat?

They love invisible things. Divinity only they can see. I've asked to look at their sketches but they refuse to show me anything, time and time again. They insist on my patience. They aren't ready yet. At this point, I don't know if they'll ever be ready. If their big gallery show is even going to happen. It's been months since they first started drawing me.

I don't care if the show happens, but I want to know what I look like to them more than anything else. I hate that I want to know. I hate how much I want it.

I DID AN ADULT PHOTO SET, but my energy was lackluster and the photographer that I usually work with called it off early. She told me to go home and gave me fifty bucks more than we agreed on. When I objected, she folded my hand around the money and said I needed the rest. Made me agree that I wouldn't call her until I worked on myself. I wanted to cry right there in her studio, but I didn't.

I wish I could feel that powerful energy that they saw moving me. I wish that I could see it. Some days I want to see it even more than I want to know how they see me. As if knowing the shape of my soul would clarify all the murk I slog through, or at least be the kind of secret that made slogging through the murk worthwhile.

It feels like everything I want right now is hidden in their sketchbook. Everything.

FOR OUR FINAL MODELING SESSION, they wanted to draw me in a different room on the college campus than the one we usually used. They gave me directions but I got lost twice, and when I arrived at the numbered auditorium, they kept giving me angry looks that made me blush.

"I got lost," I explained.

"I don't have this room for very long," they said. "Just an hour."

When I entered, I realized that it wasn't just an auditorium; there was a raised wooden stage bordered with red curtains at the bottom of the tiered plush seating. This was one of the theater department's stages.

"Go on the stage," they said.

I shivered. Descended the narrow path of stairs between the

seats to the bottom. A spotlight went on, highlighting the gold of the polished wooden boards. I looked back but couldn't see them behind the flare of the spotlight. I disrobed in the shadows just offstage, hesitated, then removed my underwear. They hadn't requested it this time, but I wanted to be as exposed to them as I possibly could be.

I mounted the stage. The wood creaked beneath me. I looked up and saw only the spotlight. I shielded my eyes, squinting at the seats.

"I'm here," they said. I couldn't see them, but they sounded close. "Start whenever you're ready."

I nodded, and began my disjointed dance. I swept my leg wide. Clenched my limbs inward like a fist. Hefted an unseen lance. Soon I could hear them join me; invisible graphite scratching across invisible paper. A duet of obstruction, connected at my hips. I thrust my hips as if I could tug them closer to me. Looked up. And saw.

A form so innately mutable it was almost indescribable, but powerful and raw, pulsing–

I fell down. The back of my head struck the solid wood of the stage. All my perception shut off, abruptly replaced with darkness. When my head rebounded and hit the wood a second time, my vision returned. They knelt over me, eclipsing the spotlight and the hideous, perfect glowing thing behind them with the limbs of a writhing star.

"Are you all right?" they asked me. "Are you hurt? Talk to me."

"I see it," I said. It loomed over us both. When it briefly enmeshed with the restless form of their soul I felt a dart of heat; they were looking at me.

"You see your arcane liquidity?" they asked. "Do you see mine?"

"Yes," I said.

"You do? Tell me! What does it look like?"

I blinked. "You can't see it?"

"No!" I shivered and they peeled their jacket off and handed it to me. "I've done everything I can to widen my spiritual apertures! I've meditated. Taken mind-altering substances. Consulted countless advisors. But I can only see the spiritual limbic of a few."

"Really?" I asked. They reached out to touch the curve of my cheek and I witnessed the fleshy, wet fabric of their soul guide their hand there. It pulsed arrhythmically. Expanded and contracted at whim.

"Yes," they said, reaching up to touch the ropey meat of my glistening soul. As their fingers connected with my ethereal tissue I cried out with pleasure. "I've only fallen in love with a few souls so far," they said, and they buried their tongue in the golden-red sinews of my arcane liquidity while I ruptured beneath them with ecstasy.

When my hips stopped automatically jittering backwards, I reached up and seized a fistful of their soul. They moaned and tumbled to the stage and I pressed my open mouth against their hidden flesh.

FISTS BANG ON THE DOOR. A key is scraped into the lock. On stage, our tangled amalgam covers us in golden, fibrous starlight. The stage is flooded with antediluvian fluids spurting from secret apertures above us. A void has formed just above our souls, ink black and gently tugging at the curtains with its cold vacuum. Their sketches are curling in the warm gore on the auditorium floor. They whisper softly into the tender whorls of my wet non-binary soul, and I am luminous, golden, burning with their love and ready for our audience.

HER SKIN A GRIM CANVAS

GWENDOLYN KISTE

You see me for the first time when I'm standing in the shadows, a drink in my hand, my heart on my sleeve.

"Are you alone?" you ask, and I blush a little and nod.

It's a morbid Saturday night in late December, and we're at a warehouse party on the South Side, the kind of artsy soiree where everybody who's anybody is dying to get in.

But part of me is dying to get out. That's because I don't belong here. I'm fresh off the bus, a girl with no past besides a grimy small town and an even grimier family. Now here I am in a new city and a new dress, pretending I fit in, pretending I didn't just bluff my way into a last-minute invitation. I'm so good at make-believe that I almost fool myself.

But you don't buy my masquerade. You peer into me as if my skin is translucent, as if I'm made of glass.

"This isn't your scene, is it?" you ask, and I feel caught beneath the impossible weight of your stare.

"No," I say. "It's not."

You glance around the room, an arcane look drifting behind your eyes. "I don't blame you," you say at last. "Sometimes, I don't know why I'm here either."

You never introduce yourself. You don't have to. Everyone already knows your name. You're an impresario, a visionary they say. A strange sort of fashion designer with a flair for the dramatic. I've seen your dresses. On the covers of glossy magazines and in the windows of upscale boutiques where the purse-lipped women at the counters never make me feel welcome. But it's worth enduring their glares, just for a moment, just to get a glimpse of what you create.

Even up close, your designs hardly look real, the angles of the shoulders sharp as daggers, the waistlines like grotesque hourglasses. Some call your clothing unwearable, but you never seem to mind. If anything, you carry critique like a badge of honor.

"Would you like to see my studio?" you ask.

"Yes," I say without thinking twice.

It takes us ten minutes in your vintage Shelby Cobra, the slick interior cold against my skin. Everything's humming in me, electric and alive. Ask anyone, and they'd tell you: this is the chance of a lifetime. A chance to become somebody. Your confidant, your muse.

I only hope they're right.

Your studio at the edge of the Strip District is a vast complex that seems to stretch for a mile. It's packed with pristine fabrics and spools of silk thread and headless dress forms like lonely ghosts, and you delight in showing me every crevice.

"This is where I do most of my work," you say matter-of-factly, as we breeze past a row of Husqvarna sewing machines and a drafting table draped in muslin mockups. You show me your boardroom and your bedroom and your showroom too with its shiny rows of chairs and a perilously thin runway. Every once in a while, you even host a small event here, private little affairs for your most devoted fans.

There's only one place where you don't take me. It's toward the back, its red door gleaming through the midnight, and as I edge closer, I swear I hear the rhythm of distant heartbeats.

"What's in there?" I want to ask, but my heart squeezes tight in my chest, and I don't speak the question aloud. I'm scared it will break the spell. Then this will all be over before it's even begun.

I turn away, and you're suddenly looming over me, so much

nearer than I expect. Without a word, you put your hand on mine, and I suddenly feel a very long way from home.

"Stay the night," you say.

For a moment, I hesitate. This only makes you laugh.

"It isn't what you think," you say, and you're right. You're interested in my body, but not in the usual way.

With a measuring tape pulled taut, you loop it around my waist and breasts and thighs, calculating the precise geometry of my body. Like I'm no more than a mathematical equation to solve. Then with a grimace, you start transposing your vision onto me, weaving satin ribbons around my throat and corseting my waist so tight I can barely breathe. My body bends, my bones constrict, but with my eyes closed, I tell myself it's all right. This is what I want. This is my ticket out, my escape from my cockroach-laden apartment across town and the dead-end desk job I took because nobody else would have me.

You work all night, your hands all over me, and when the first wink of dawn steals through the window, you finally look me in the eye and smile.

"You're perfect," you whisper.

I blush and smile back.

YOU INVITE me to stay longer—a day, a night, a week—and then you invite me to stay for good.

"It'll be easier with you here," you say, and I move in my things, more than happy to trade roaches for riches.

I expect it to be just the two of us, working together, unlikely collaborators, partners in crime, but you're never alone, not really. There are always accountants and assistants, swarming around you like worker bees. They're not surprised to see me here, the stranger in their midst. It's almost as if they were expecting me. The new muse. The girl you'll elevate to greatness.

The weeks blur by, as you stitch me a dozen outfits, maybe even a hundred, bolts of bright taffeta and red satin and silk the color of cornflower unfurling over the curves of my body. But no matter how beautiful I think the dresses are, none of them is quite right, at least not according to you.

"It needs to fit you better," you keep saying. "It needs to be part of you."

I shift and pose and do my best, but I can see it there in your gaze, how I'm suddenly not perfect anymore.

"I'm sorry," I whisper, but you say nothing in return.

MY FIRST FASHION show is on a Thursday night in the arts district. The runway's made of glass, and it feels like I'll slip right through the cracks if I'm not careful.

"Don't worry," you say. "You'll be fine."

I smile at you, desperate to prove you right. Except this doesn't go the way I expect. I'm the only model in your show, rushing backstage and changing, quick as lightning.

"Is this how it's usually done?" I ask your assistants, but they snuff at me.

"Hurry up," they say and yank a pale leather sheath over my head.

I want to argue with them. I want to tell them no. But I do as they say, and I do it well, gliding down the runway like a swan, like the perfection you demand of me.

At the after party, I expect a real celebration. A glorious fete in your honor and mine. Only the moment the lights come up, it's like I no longer exist. Your ardent fans won't look me in the eye, won't look at me at all. You don't look at me either, too rapt in their adoration to bother.

I slink back against the wall, alone all over again, and when everyone thinks I'm not listening, they all whisper of the muses that came before me. Who they were, how I measure up. I've never seen any of the girls in person, but sometimes, I sneak glimpses of them in the stacks of old magazines and photo negatives you keep tucked away in dusty drawers. They were beautiful —of course, they were. You'd tolerate nothing less.

The next morning, we're back to work, my body shaking, a glare on your face. I was hoping for an afterglow, that you could take a moment to savor last night's success, but I'm not so fortunate.

"This isn't right," you say and toss up your hands.

I shrink into the corner. It's easy to figure out what I should do. I should leave right now. I should walk out on you. But where am I supposed to go? Back to an apartment I no longer have or the family I no longer want? I've given up everything to be here. All for a chance to be graced with your glory.

"What can I do?" I ask at last.

You pace back and forth, running your fingers through your dark hair. "I need to try something different."

"Anything," I say, and instantly, I regret it, because a strange look clouds your eyes.

I start to back away, but you carefully thread your sharpest needle, and I know I've already agreed to this.

"It'll only hurt a little," you promise, and I do my best not to wince as the metal pierces my thin skin. You loop it in and out of me, over and over, and I can feel the silk thread become one with my flesh.

"Why?" My voice no more than a whisper.

"It's the only way," you say, and I nod, doing my best to believe you.

THIS SOON BECOMES OUR RITUAL. You with a needle and a handful of notions, attaching little bits here and there. A zipper on my back, a satin bow beneath the small of my neck, a piece of lace stitched into my thigh like a ghoulish garter belt.

They say you have to suffer for your art. So that's exactly what I'll do.

Except you're still never happy. "Let's try again," you say, and with a seam ripper against my skin, you rend my flesh like it's nothing. Like *I'm* nothing, just another piece of cheap muslin.

"It's almost over," you say when you've only just started, and I force a smile through the tears.

This is the only way you know how to touch me now. Like I'm a convict at the gallows, and you're my gleeful executioner.

As you sketch out your next design, my momentary reprieve, I curl up in bed, my body raw and aching, and thumb through old magazines filled with your past designs. And your past muses. I try to memorize their faces. The redhead with a splash of freckles on the tip of her nose. The girl with hair the color of midnight and lips painted red as a pomegranate. The shy one who never looks at the camera, not even when the flash must have been so close it was blinding.

The articles never say where the muses went afterward. There's no goodbye shows for them, no farewell interviews. They simply vanish, swapped out with someone new, an endless daisy chain of beautiful girls.

"What happened to them?" I ask, doing my best not to glance toward the darkened room where we never go.

You watch me quietly, a needle and thread in your hand. "Do you really want to know?" you ask, and I shake my head.

ANOTHER EVENING, another show. Your assistants bustle back and forth, the spotlights flickering overhead, everyone tittering about what you have in store for them. Meanwhile, we stand together backstage, and you stitch roses across my shoulders, never bothering to remove the thorns as you bury the stems deep within my flesh.

"Aren't you perfect?" you murmur, but I won't listen. I simply wait until you're finished. Then I creep off by myself and peer between the velvet curtains out into the audience. Your devotees are crowding into their seats now. They don't want to miss your latest exhibition.

"Such great work," they say to you afterward, pushing past me like I'm air, thin streams of red still trickling down my arms.

Around midnight, we retreat to your studio where you keep working, your brow knit, your hands rough. Next to you, I fold my arms into my chest and stare at the locked room in the corner.

"Are you all right?" you ask from the drafting table.

I shake my head and think how this should be different. There should be a blood-stained key and a warning never to cross the threshold. You should at least try to hide what you've done. Instead, you smile and take me by the hand.

"It's time," you say, as you unlock the door and flick on the light, a single bare bulb that bathes the narrow room in jaundiced yellow. But it's more than enough to see them.

Sometimes, you already know the answer without ever asking the question.

They're positioned upright in glass cases, their blank eyes staring out like lost mannequins, their bodies raw and carved out, the same as mine. I recognize their faces, each of them wearing a final design from you.

The freckled redhead with rubies embedded around both wrists like bracelets. Or shackles.

The black-haired muse with an onyx pendant branded between her breasts.

The shy one who you probably especially loved to put on display. Her entire body is speckled with a thousand rhinestones, thick rows of them up and down and between her thighs. Even now, her face is twisted with what you did to her.

I press my shaking palms into the glass, as if I might still rescue them. "What have you done?"

"Given them eternal life," you say, but we both know that's a lie. This isn't life. It's not even death. It's something in between, the worst of both worlds. I listen for their heartbeats but all I can hear is my own, throbbing in my ears like a siren.

I stay with them, whispering, trying to coax them back, as you stand beside me, chuckling. Midnight dissolves into day, and when it's clear they won't awaken, you usher me back out the door, locking it up behind us. Soon, your assistants arrive at their desks and sewing machines, pretending this is like every other morning. But nothing is the same now. Do they know all about your muses? Is that why they won't look me in the eye? Or do they simply not want to think about where the other women have gone?

And if I speak the truth about you, if I spit it out like fire, they won't believe me, will they? No matter how many times they claim they will, no matter how often people say that it matters, that forgotten girls like me matter. But they only give a damn if the truth doesn't inconvenience them too much.

And let's face it: truth is rarely as convenient as silence.

That night, there's another fashion show in the arts district. Another crowd ready for me to entertain them. I wait for a lighting designer to distract you with a random question before I sneak off to a back office and make a call, dialing a number I struggle to remember.

"Hello?" the gravelly voice on the other end answers.

"Mom?" I whisper, and for a moment, I'm sure it's not too late.

"Who is this?" she asks, her words like snake venom. "Why are you bothering me?"

Then it all comes flooding back. The reason I ran in the first place. All those dirty houses with dirty mattresses, and the hungry faces with fists always bunched up and looking for somebody to blame.

My hand quivering, I hang up the phone. There's no place for me to go. Nowhere left to run. No home, no family, no sympathetic ear that might believe me. You possess all the keys to the world and all the locks too. If this were like the fairy tale, my brother or my mother would burst in any minute and rescue me from you. But I have no saviors. I only have myself, and it turns out that's not enough.

On the runway, I do my best imitation of what you want me to be. A Frankenstein's monster, an amalgam of a girl. In the audience, they're watching me, the wolves they are, their teeth glistening, ready to devour my body whole. You're serving me up to them on a silver platter, and from backstage, your dark gaze peering out at me, you love every minute of it. The way I belong to you. The way you can parade me as your own.

Afterward, you strip the latest design from me and box it up for some millionaire philanthropist's wife from Palm Springs.

"But it's ruined," I say, my fingers sliding over dark crusts of my blood on the collar. "You can't sell that to her."

"Of course I can sell it," you say with a scoff. "That's why they want it in the first place. For those special little details."

Everything in me goes cold. They know what you're doing—to me, to the others before—and they like it. They revel in it. This rich lady in her rich home probably won't ever wear the dress. She just wants to collect it.

To collect the broken pieces of me.

Rage rises up the back of my throat, and I want to rip all your devotees to shreds and then do the same to you. Except I can't imagine how I possibly could. One girl against an unspeakable crowd.

We drive back to your studio, and I don't say a word, my throat dry, my heart empty. Were the other muses like me? Did they have no safe place to go? If so, you probably looked like a prince to them, a savior eager to wrap them in satin. And to suffocate them in it too.

You loom over me for hours, always reminding me not to move as you do your work. "This isn't right," you sneer and bury the needle deeper than you've ever gone before, your fingers dipping so far into me I'm afraid you'll tear me in two.

"Please stop," I say, but you don't listen as you pierce through my muscle, scratching through bone. Shuddering, I close my eyes and press my ear into the wall. There it is again. An uncanny chorus of heartbeats.

"Are you still here?" I whisper to them.

You shake your head. "They're long gone," you say, never giving them a chance to answer.

The same way I'll be gone too, dissolved like sea foam in the ocean.

Ask anyone, and they'd tell you: this is still the chance of a lifetime. To be cut up by a genius, turned into his scraps. After all, you're a visionary. That word reserved for a man like you. The rest of us are merely lucky to be noticed at all.

I'm lucky. That's what they'd say.

You find me resting by a window, my flesh still bright pink and oozing from your latest design. "We have a show tonight."

I stare up at you, my chest aching. "Already?"

"Don't worry," you say. "We're hosting it here. It'll be an easy one, I promise."

As though anything about this is easy. Especially one of your private events, the kind with only a few of your favorites in attendance. I've only heard about these special shows before. I don't even know what's so different about them. As you make plans for the evening, I creep behind you and eavesdrop.

"No photographers tonight," you say on the phone, and my heart squeezes tight as I realize it: it's the last show, *my* last show. The finale of me. My so-called imperfections have taken their toll of you. For all these months, I've been no more than a product for you to slice and dice and distribute to the highest bidder.

Now I'm just a trend that went out of style.

I try to gather my things quietly, try to think of how I'll run, but your admirers are already crowding into the studio, pushing me back. I press into the walls like a rat and keep moving, but you spot me first. Grinning, you corner me by your drafting table, and before I have time to scream, you take your eyelet pliers and embed a row of diamonds around my throat, like a parting gift from a lover.

"You'll be my masterpiece," you whisper, and I'm sure that's what you tell all the girls.

I try again to run, but your assistants circle me like vultures. They zip me into a suede dress, and with the music pulsing in the speakers, drowning out my cries, they push me in front of the audience. That's when I see it there beneath the spotlight.

A glass coffin awaiting me at the end of the runway. You're

waiting there too with your needle and thread, ready to stitch up my heart until it goes quiet in my chest.

I turn wildly in circles, searching every direction. The exits are blocked, the incandescent lights overhead too blinding to run. The only thing I see from here is that across the studio, the red door to your secret room is already unlocked for me. I'll join your other muses tonight. This destiny you've designed for me.

But first, you'll put me to work. I have a dozen dresses to model, and you expect me to merrily display each one. I take my time on the runway, trying to stall, to do anything to stop this.

On the last outfit, as your assistants argue over who gets to watch from the audience as you put the finishing touches on me, I slip away into the unlocked room.

Inside, the heartbeats are growing louder now. Your muses are waiting to be woken up. This is a fairy tale after all. Only there will be no true love's kiss this time. We learned that lesson the hard way: there isn't an iota of affection in you.

But if we can't have love, maybe we can try something else. Maybe rage will work just as well.

With the music still blaring, I draw back my fist and bring it down on their transparent coffins. The glass shatters around them, a broken spell, a broken promise, and with a careful hand, I reach into their vivisected chests and yank free the heavy threads you stitched into them.

Then I hold my breath, as one by one, your muses open their eyes.

"Hello," I whisper.

They smile back at me. "Hello," they say in unison.

I guide them out of the room, and together, we parade down the runway, our bodies a bitter roadmap of what you've done to us. Of what we've survived.

The music cuts out suddenly, and silence settles over the audience, their mouths gaping, their eyes wide and afraid. Then we descend into the crowd, our teeth exposed, our hands curled into claws.

It's strange how quickly the silence gives way to screams.

As your fans turn to pulp in our hands, you do your best to

run, hiding behind your dress forms and drafting papers, but you don't make it far. We save you for last. We savor what we do to you.

And when we're through, we'll don your skin like lace and leather, and with our scarred hands entwined, we'll slip into the waiting midnight, laughing together because we'll never be alone again.

THE DEEP END OF YOU

HAILEY PIPER

THERE IS NO ONE IN THE WORLD LIKE YOU EXCEPT YOU.

That's what Green and Ember told you when they brought you to their studio. At least, it's someone's studio. You don't know who owns this white unfurnished chamber, but they have an easier time saying it's theirs, same as their convenient monikers. Green with her mint-colored mohawk pulled up from a pale scalp; Ember with her red fiery fluff over bronze.

Whoever they are, whoever owns this studio, they're paying, so you're here. Ember stands behind an easel where a thick sketchbook clipped to the drawing board lets her scrawl charcoal and pencil unseen.

You sit empty-handed on a raised stage-like platform, a little nervous, a lot unclothed. Green perches behind you, coating oil over your bare back like she's greasing an uncooperative wheel before a journey while she slides encouraging whispers into your ear.

"Hands clasped, look to Ember, hands clasped, don't look down, look at Ember, you're doing amazing, hands clasped."

You're half-listening, half-lost in memory, trying to recall what Ember said when this session began. The studio has no windows, only the stern wooden door where Green and Ember led you inside, but it must still be night outside. Not much time has passed, right? Too little for you to have grown fruit in your once-empty hands.

And yet a red apple sits between your fingers. You haven't looked down—you're behaving, a good model for Ember's art—but you feel the weight on your palms, the crisp skin beneath your thumbs. If you push hard, you can dent and bruise the surface, and the flesh would turn earthen beneath.

Green's gasp in your ear makes you jolt and cast your eyes down. Only a flicker, but in that instant you spy the apple. It wasn't there before.

It isn't there now. You blink, and it's gone, and you hurry your gaze back to Ember before she or Green realize you've disobeyed.

They don't seem to have noticed. Green works with you, Ember captures the act.

Another gasp flutters behind your ear. Warm breath follows it. You almost look back, but you don't want to defy Green's encouragement again.

Her teeth clack together. "I'm with you," she says. "We're in this together, our visages in Ember's hands."

You're together on the platform in skin-to-skin contact, but you're not really in this together, are you? Green isn't your girl-friend, and Ember didn't find the two of you. They came together. Green is more Ember's collaborator, even as her oil-slick fingers dance over your naked shoulders and across your collarbone. You tense your chest against a gasp of your own, unsure if you're supposed to react or enjoy this. When her hands dive deeper across sensitive nipples, you can't hide an uncoiling shudder down your spine. Your head tilts back, exposing your throat.

It's not complete disobedience—you're not looking at Ember, sure, but you're not looking down again either. You're looking up, at the world above you, at Green.

At the face of a horned goat. Close enough to count the chin hair, to feel hot breath and take in the curve of the horns.

You crumple forward and scream, ducking your head beneath your hands. Green's fingers withdraw from your chest, your shoulders. You feel her crouching beside you, hear her calling your name and asking, "What's wrong?"

A pencil clacks on the hard floor, followed by a clatter of boot-steps. Ember leans against the platform's edge and pries a hand from your head.

"What did you see?" she asks.

You tell her about the non-existent apple first, as if that matters. You then mention the goat, which stood where Green stands, but there's nothing else here, only you and her. She stares into Ember until Ember hurries back to her easel and tears away the top page. When she brings it to the platform, you look, as if Green is still urging you to gaze ahead.

But you wish you hadn't.

There's a perfect black-and-white depiction of you upon the platform, on your knees, hands clasped, eyes staring out from the drawing. The only inconsistency between the art of you and reality is the apple in your charcoal hands.

Green's depiction stands further off the mark. While the picture shows her hands slathering your body with oil, her torso remains unbent and upright. Another pair of arms break from her shoulders, raised to either side as if welcoming a pencil-drawn rain.

Her mohawk is gone, replaced by curved horns atop her goatish head.

"No way she could've seen," Ember says.

Green beams. "It's working."

A nervous joy flits butterfly-like beneath their expressions, but they're not too distracted to forget you. Both sets of eyes fall to yours, two blues, two hazels.

"You're shaking," Green says. "Let's take five, yeah?"

OUTSIDE THE CHAMBER, the world is drywall and linoleum, and the glass windows frame a gloomy parking lot beneath a starless night sky. You find the restroom and have a cry, a terror piss, and a breather to check yourself in the mirror. You're naked beneath a thick crimson robe, but you've been naked in tougher situations.

Remember, it could be worse. You're at a three-way fork in your personal road, with no way to pay on rent, groceries, or student loans this week, or at least you were before this night began. Green and Ember are paying you to be here, and that matters. Better company with these two money-bound oddists or occultists or whatever they like to be called than back at the bar with Randolph and Jackson, playfighting over who gets to buy you another unemployment pity drink, and then fighting for real over who gets to take you home.

"You won't hit me," Jackson said earlier tonight. "You're just a boy."

"And you're nothing but a yappy dog," Randolph slurred, raising fists. "Still, we're going to do this like men."

You had no idea what movie either of them thought they were in, and you didn't stick around for the climax, let alone the end credits where both men likely landed ass-first on the street.

Green surprised you, arm in arm with Ember. Both wore smiles on their faces as if they expected to find you outside the bar, and they had their explanation of art projects and payment all lined up. Someone in your social circle must have tipped Green off that you'd been fired from Patterson's. You'd probably started the word down the grapevine while sucking down a sympathetic margarita.

"How comfortable are you naked?" Ember asked. "All the way?"

You never had to answer a question like that before.

Green popped in. "We need someone deep. Do you understand? There are so few truly deep people in the world. In fact, there is no one in the world like you." She reached out to one side.

Ember grasped her hand. "Will you be that depth for us?"

You wanted to be. It warmed you to be told you were special. You had one other question for them though, inklings of instinct held tight since the days of listening for signals your parents were about to fight, a wariness for school kids about to hurt you. Life's eternal lesson—best watch out for yourself, because no one else will.

"Is it dangerous?" you asked.

"Not for you," Green said, quickly.

That was enough to bring you here, before appearing/disappearing apples and Green growing a goat's head and horns because a picture told her to. These weird sensations make you wonder what exactly is in the oil Green's been soaking into your skin. Some kind of drug? A poison? Were someone to lick you, would they die of your toxins? All for some hellish art project.

No matter where you go or who you're with, it seems there's always a battle.

The restroom door cracks open, and Ember's red hair precedes her. "Ready for more?"

You don't answer in words, but you follow her.

BACK TO THE STERN DOOR, the chamber, the platform where Green helps you up and coils you into her limbs. Her hands are still slick with oil.

"More challenging angles this time," Ember says from behind her easel. "Let it be pictured; let it be so."

Your robe falls away as Green's hands again run down your shoulders and creep toward your chest. She whispers for you to watch Ember, see her fingers coated by charcoal and graphite. A studious greed powers her eyes as she recreates you on paper.

This time, watching her is no struggle. You're curious what exactly she's drawing now. How much of her art will depict you and Green upon the platform? How much will deviate? Is there a difference when every artist molds the perceptions of real life through the lens of their art, and is that any different than what people choose to see, and not see, through their own eyes? Memory is imperfect, a fragment of perception.

Like art.

Green's hands pass your chest and cross at the wrists over your belly. You aren't sure how far down she expects to go, but you can't help a glance this time.

Turquoise patterns swirl down her skin. You think they must

form thin writing, a kind of tattoo, but they're too plentiful to have gone outside your notice before.

Your eyes flick back to Ember. Has she drawn these markings on Green? What dictates the vibrant color when the art is black and white?

Green's hands splay over your waist, and then she unfolds her wrists as if her hands are opening double doors.

A chasm gasps inside you. You feel it suck at the underside of your skin, a greedy mouth about to drop your flesh down some unseen pit. Ember and Green said you were deep before, but you hadn't realized how much, and no one until now has treated you in a way to make you think so.

But there must be a far-reaching pit in your guts or heart or somewhere. Wind whistles down its throat, as if it has been covered all your life and only tonight has taken the chance to open.

You bite your lip to keep silent and then realize you'll never forgive yourself if you don't speak now.

"You said it wasn't dangerous for me," you whisper.

"Why would it be?" Green asks.

You have no answer. A funny feeling inside? You like the idea that you're special and deep, but maybe you're too special? Too deep? Somewhere down that inner pit lies a suspicion that Green and Ember are hiding something.

"Please," Green says. "We need you. There's no one in the world like you."

You wish you knew what that meant. Something to do with your body, the pit inside, or your mind? Nothing's clear anymore. You let her hands work down your abdomen, fingers plucking your nerves like the strings of an organic lute, like she might coax you into relaxed pleasure. It almost works.

But you tilt your head back, and the horned goat stares down, its strange eyes offering oblong darkness where two dark blobs seem to hold hands.

You jerk your head down. "We need to stop."

Hot breath rushes past your ear. "We're making terrific

progress." It should be Green—it sounds like Green—but it's not quite Green.

"I don't want to do this anymore," you say, to whoever or whatever will listen.

"But you want to pay your student loans and rent," the Green-like voice says. "You want to eat, don't you?"

That three-way fork of misery stretches through your mind. You focus again on Ember and her easel, imagining the goat head she must have drawn in place of Green's. How many limbs does it have this time? What else will change in the picture? On the platform?

In you?

Your eyelids stiffen, and you count how many seconds you stare between blinks. Eleven at first, because you're thinking too hard about it. And then twenty seconds. Thirty. You manage forty-five before your eyes water. Goat whiskers tickle your ear, and you blink hard, shudder, and then stare ahead again, as if watching Ember will stop the night, as if averting your gaze from the changes means they aren't happening.

As if you have any control of your life.

When has that ever been the case? Remember when you were that kid who tried to keep your parents from fighting? They'd only argue worse, no different than the boys at the bar. And when you tried to keep your head down at school, that would only draw the hellspawn to your scent.

Everywhere, everyone, a battle. You've never had a say. Never taken a stand. Every job, you've been the one fired, never the one who quits. Every relationship, you've been dumped, never the one who dumps. Is there really a three-way fork of misery in your future, or do they all loop back onto the same broken highway? Would you know the difference even if signposts marked the off-road ditch every couple miles?

The pit within doesn't answer, but you can always try. Your hand twitches at the beginning of choice—you can disrupt the reality of Ember's drawing by removing your body from her sight. Fingers grope for the robe and draw it toward your body. You brush away Green's still-human hands.

"You can't," she says. "We need you. There's—"

"I know," you say. "There's no one in the world like me. But that's too bad."

Your legs tense as you begin to rise. You're finally making a decision for yourself, and maybe fate will be kind in return. A detour might open, an exit, even a trail of matted grass carved by wildlife. There can be other directions in life besides those handed to you, and you'll find them outside this room, somewhere in the night.

If only you could get up.

Your legs are no longer the firm limbs of bone and toned sinew that carried you out of the bar earlier tonight. They're limp, toeless wads of flesh, like grand slugs stretching from your thighs. Your arms, too, have gone boneless from the elbows down. Your fingers have fused into awkward lumps. There's a hardness to their ends, and you wonder if these are your knuckles or the forming of hooves.

"You can't go," Green says. "We have to keep you. We've learned we have no choice."

Hard surfaces clack down the chamber, and you turn from your traitorous limbs to the easel, and Ember. She's placed her hands around her ream of paper, and she's midway through turning the easel so you can see what she's made of you.

"Did you really think you were the first?" Ember asks. "That we've perfected the technique all in one night? We've been so close before."

Your test your lips, tongue, jaw—all still yours. "Let me go," you say. "If you've done it before, you can find someone else."

"Weren't you listening? There's no one in the world like you." Ember raises her pencil, deadlier than a pistol. "Because when they tried to walk, we stopped them. You're all that's left, and we're too close to move on. Now slide back into Green's arms. She's cold and lonely."

It isn't your choice to return to Green's embrace; she lays her hands on your chest again. Coarse hair brushes your spine, and you wonder how goatish she's become, why that particular animal might be important. Something about the eyes, the way their pupils resemble figures with clasped hands, their echo of a divided world.

You catch glimpses of the art ahead, in the momentary gaps where Ember's torso and limbs give way to the paper and its cursed drawing. There, a curved horn. In the corner, a sluggish former leg.

Other shapes surround you and Green in the picture, odd angles and crude markings in the same swirly patterns as decorate Green's skin. There are gaps in the paper, too, as if Ember has drawn another artist into the picture who likewise blocks and reveals sections of the drawing with her body.

The same gaps open beyond the easel. You feel one inside, don't you? And look out the corner of your eye—there's another, a breach in the studio's white wall.

A swirling blue hall opens where there has never been a door, at least that you could see. Indiscernible figures wander a path in the darkness, their midnight-blue robes flaring behind them, their white masks never glancing your way, as if you and Green and Ember are the bizarre sight and they are travelers walking their own doomed road. You wonder if they'll find a three-way fork ahead.

Another breach slides open in a shadowy corner near the studio's exit. And then another parts its lips in the wall near the platform.

Ember's pencil turns brutal against the paper's corners, a hurricane of crosshatching shadows and dark smears. The more furious her strokes, the more friction blurs and distorts the studio's edges, as if the entire world were one great sketchbook ravaged by an artist caught between brilliance and madness.

"It's time," Green whispers.

"Almost," Ember says.

Green's hands rise beside your head. They also remain upon your chest and belly. She must have four of them, maybe more. Some might wander the room unseen, helping Ember to stretch open the world.

"We're ready," Green says. "I feel it."

Last chance. You flop your dead-fish limbs on the platform, hoping for some detour off this universal page. Reality to art, art to reality—none of it matters outside this room. That must be why they've chosen it. You're only one person they found on the street; this shouldn't be your problem.

But it isn't your choice either. Unique as you are, it was never about what you wanted. Nothing ever has been.

"Now, my love!" Green shouts, and you think you hear bleating beneath her voice.

"Yes," Ember hisses.

She curls her fist around her pencil, raises it high over her head, and stabs knife-like into the drawing. You catch another glimpse of the worlds she's opened at the page's edges—heavenly bodies in space, paths through strange nothingness, an infinity divided by triangles and eyes.

And then her stained fingers dig into the paper and shred it from the center, tearing open both the art and the world.

It gasps around you, the sudden light shocked to find this mundane room thrown into its splendor. The opening draws from the torn edges around you, but also it gapes from the pit you never knew stretched within your body, your soul. The depth you cherished, and the others craved.

You are open now, like you never have been. Had Green and Ember found you years ago and worked subtly at this chasm within, maybe your openness would have spilled honesty into the world. No more trying to please parents, employers, peers, lovers—you would have told them how you felt, and maybe they would have run, or maybe they would have wanted you. Loved you.

But that road lies far behind.

You're here instead, where Green's goat-head has returned to its vibrant mohawk and human shape, where Ember's bootsteps storm through the studio, onto the platform, into a light so thick it runs river-like from your belly. If the world is paper, you're the bridge between one side of the sheet and the other, and the whole thing is folding around as if you're both inside and outside yourself. A thousand edges, many thousand sides to some cosmic papery shape.

You've become a sucking wound, and reality won't suffer you for the length of time those parents, employers, peers, and lovers suffered you. Everything is open; everything is closing.

"Hands clasped," Green says.

"Don't look down," Ember says.

Two heavy stones make to drop into your river—Green and Ember, clasping each other's hands. At a surface-level touch, you glean a surface-level understanding. There's something in the world they want to escape, and this might be their way off that road. There's also something in the beyond they want to reach, and they're going through you to get it.

Fixing the rip lies outside their power or yours; the world will close this wound on its own. There's little time left to decide anything, and your image has already been determined by Ember's broken drawing.

But not their images. Ember may have jellied your limbs, but she and Green haven't broken your willpower. Fate may offer a fork in its path for them, too.

You've never had a say. Take a stand now. If you can't win the battle, make a stalemate.

As Green and Ember slip into your doorway's waters, you stretch your spine the way you did when Green's fingers danced pleasantly down your skin. The doorway twists with muscle and flesh.

And it twists against Green, the more malleable of the couple. Ripples surge through your river, and she's thrown one way while Ember sinks elsewhere.

They have one frozen moment to realize their hands have come unclasped, no stronger than two slugs seeking each other in the dark, and then Ember drifts one way, Green another. Both vanish into the blue-folded currents without so much as a thanks or a scream.

You can't really blame them. You're about to do the same. At least they won't enjoy what's to come any more than you will.

Reality's page finishes folding, pushing you into yourself until you erupt out the far side of your doorway. You should be torn inside-out, but instead you're plummeting into the thick light. The breaches you glimpsed in Ember's art and from the platform ripple open, but none of them show the studio, the stern door, the hallway, the windows to the parking lot and the familiar night.

There is no one in the world like you anymore. Not even you.

LUCIO

ROLAND BLACKBURN

SHE WOULD NOT CALL HIM MAESTRO.

It would have been the smart thing for Celia to say on her first visit to the studio, even if Lucio Frazzi would have demurred. But at the last second, she balked.

We're making midnight movies, not a damn opera.

Instead, she half-bowed, half-curtsied, unaware of what was appropriate on this side of the Atlantic. Frazzi waved it away, studying her with his one good eye.

The middle-aged director was shorter than she'd thought, but no less commanding. A natty Bohemian with steely hair poking out from beneath his black flat cap, he mumbled a quick something at Rosso.

Rosso replied, his sneer melting to a full-on grimace. Since the go-between had picked her up from the Peretola airport two hours ago, he'd asked her to refer to Frazzi as *Maestro* no less than a dozen times. Almost as many times as she'd had to slap his hand off her ass.

Celia knew it was going to be a long two weeks.

This was Italian Hollywood, after all.

But it was a chance to go from Z-movies to B-s.

Alphabet climbing.

And if it meant she'd get to knee some wannabe in the balls, so much the better.

"The maestro welcomes you to Tiberius Studio. If there's anything you need to make yourself more comfortable, you ask."

Celia glanced around the workspace. Beside the heavy tables and racks upon racks of latex, plasters, and paints, they had thrown an ill-used cot in the corner and a battered nightstand for her things. Her tour had only revealed the set mock-ups for *The Outside,* the odd workspace, and prop storage. Hers was the first sleeping arrangement she'd seen.

On the ride over, she'd tried hardlining Rosso about getting a hotel. He'd only laughed, inviting her to spend two hours in a suite downtown.

This is how we do things, he'd said.

This is how we make the magic happen.

This is a boy's club.

"It's an honor, Mr. Frazzi."

Rosso winced, not bothering to translate.

Frazzi said something else and chuckled, his one good eye twinkling beside the black eyepatch that obscured the other.

If you'd listened to Nonna back in Dayton, you'd be speaking Italian right alongside them.

Rosso snorted. "You're short. Is good."

Prickling, Celia started to say something, but Frazzi raised a silencing hand, gesturing at the workspace, the molds, the latex. Rosso translated. "You know why you're here?"

As if she'd caught a flight to Florence on a whim.

As if she couldn't be bothered to keep a thought in her pretty little head.

"You need help with the gore effects."

"But why?"

She blushed, hating herself for it. "Dario liked my work."

Rosso shook his head. "Karina McNall. She quit."

At the mention of her name, Frazzi tore off his cap and punted a wooden stool, sending it crashing against the metal racks.

Celia winced. "What?"

"Do you know nothing?"

She had seen most of Frazzi's *oeuvre,* admittedly only at midnight double features. *Seven Tombstones and a Raven. The*

Mansion by the Graveyard. Don't Torment a Platypus. The Grandfather of Gore was a legend, at least among a certain crowd.

It's why you're here, right?

Karina McNall had been the lead actor in Frazzi's last two movies, the current production concluding the de facto trilogy. *Doors to Beyond*, or something like that. She was blonde, gorgeous, and the sole competent actor, an American the director used for international appeal.

And the things she'd put up with: bleeding eyes, lost fingers, torn throat. She'd been thrown from a roof, buried in a coffin full of worms, and had a maggot tornado blown at her. The woman must have had monastic patience, and if even *she* had finally quit-

-

"Her scenes. They were never finished." Rosso threw a sympathetic glance back at Frazzi, who wrung his cap between his hands. "Including her death."

"My condolences. Why?"

The director murmured and waved his hand.

"She--did not care for the script changes." Rosso said the last like an inside joke, running a hand through his longish hair, but no one smiled. "Which is why he needs you."

Frazzi gestured to the worktable at the end of the room. As Celia drew nearer, she saw them.

Binders full of photographs. The actress shot at every conceivable angle. Long shots. Close-ups. Body-specific.

Her chin. Her forehead. Her teeth.

As she rifled through them, many centered only on the eyes.

Her migraine thundered to life.

No.

Impossible.

The director rambled to his assistant for almost a full minute. She only caught two words.

Savini.

Ohio.

"You will make a mask. A cast, both so lifelike as to deceive the eye. And the final set-piece--"

"What she wouldn't do?" Her mouth was on autopilot, her mind already reeling.

For the first time, Frazzi smiled.

Rosso sighed. "To throw herself from the balcony. Impale herself on a fencepost."

"That's not so bad."

"Between her legs."

"Oh."

Fucking men.

"And skewer her eyes on tree branches. She didn't care for the--penetration."

I should mace you.

"You want me to make a cast of someone's face. Someone who's not here."

"And mask. You are an artist, no?"

"It can't be done."

"Dario says differently. That you are a sorceress with the brush."

Both men stared at her. She felt her career tottering.

Celia chewed her lower lip thoughtfully.

This is it, kid. Your big break.

You want to stay in Dayton forever?

"When can I start?"

THEY SET her workspace up with a projector and a middle-aged operator, whose three functions appeared to be ogling her, chain smoking, and feeding reels into the machine.

Celia watched the rough footage with notepad in hand, the faintest hints of a migraine still churning. She'd already begun sketching the models for McNall, breaking down the contours of the actor's high cheekbones and proud chin, but her eyes--

There was something elusive there, some raw quality in the aquamarine that compelled attention even in the unpolished clips. She could see why Lucio had been so taken with her. Even Celia was developing a fascination.

The plot, for what little interest had been paid to it, appeared to revolve around a resurrected warlock, a requisite portal, and Karina their sole descendant. Frazzi's daughter, India, played the supporting role with a nepotistic amount of screen time, and Celia was shocked that it appeared to be set in Louisiana.

Had they been stateside?

There were plenty of night shots, characters with pancaked gore looming from the shadows in crumbling cemeteries. The dead warlock drove people to madness, then rammed them against protruding nails, glass, and even in one memorable scene a religious icon. Throats were slit, eyes gouged, and skulls somehow crushed by hand. A character vomited up what appeared to be their entire chest cavity in a stunning tribute to Frazzi's disregard for anatomy.

The effects were fabulously grotesque, and the disturbances piled on.

What's more, Celia was startled at how many close-ups there were of the actors' eyes.

Staring.

Reacting.

Glaring.

Screaming.

Without a narrative to follow, the film began to grind her down.

Some of the scenes provided were soundless, others in full-on ADR. That wasn't uncommon in Italian films, she knew. Scenes were shot in silence so the crew could tear apart and build sets, saving cost and time, but what surprised her was the resultant lack of effort. Mouths flapped as if the actors were gumming peanut butter, and she wondered if they were even trying to say their lines.

Out of all of them, McNall was the only one who didn't seem to be phoning it in.

But the discordant elements grew stranger. In some exterior shots, random animal sounds had been added, monkeys screeching in the bayou. Some of the signs in the interior shots were clear fabrications when studied, the most obvious being *DO NOT ENTRY*. Characters operated on a bizarre dream-logic that sent them careening off in the least likely directions.

Rather than making the film absurd, however, she found it unnerving. The film had the disorienting effect of a nightmare, the sense that something awful was happening without being able to describe why.

She wasn't--

Celia glanced back at the operator, who had produced a bottle of Moretti and was starting to replay the opening scenes. She was about to ask him to stop before she glimpsed something beyond him.

Blonde hair, drifting past in the darkness.

The door shutting behind her.

Of course Celia recognized the woman.

She'd spent the last two hours studying that face.

Rosso bustled into the room through the same door, waving a hand at the operator to kill the projector. "You have seen it?"

"Yeah." Head pounding, Celia tried to be objective. "The eye gouges in the hotel and crypts are a little sloppy, and India's cast for the organ-hemorrhaging is awful. If you'd be willing to reshoot, I can clean those up, make--"

"Do not tell Frazzi." Scowling, Rosso glanced behind him. "Perhaps India--"

She walked him through the gag, refining the cast and scaling back the viscera. "I mean, it's why you brought me here, right?"

He stared at her for a moment, considering. "How do you feel?"

"Migraine." A dull thunder ground against her temples like broken glass, and she popped two aspirin in front of him, dry swallowing. "Discomfited. Kind of gross."

"Ah. The beauty of the Maestro."

"The *director*. Who seems to think that the human body consists of ninety-percent red paste." Celia's father had been a medic in the Korean War, and some of the keepsakes he'd stored in the attic had fascinated her, even as a child. Bashing Frazzi's imagery wasn't going to further her career options, but there had been something so off-putting about the violence, so extreme that it was either mock it or accept a week of sleepless nights. "You guys realize there aren't monkeys in Louisiana?"

"Cute. The little conductor, telling the maestro how to play." Rosso pressed closer, looming over her on the stool. Trying not to gag at the overpowering stench of Brut wafting off his leather jacket, Celia resisted the urge to retreat. "Do not question. His is the unsettling touch. Disparate elements seep into his films like slow poison. Out of sequence, they are mere sufferings, but when placed in line--alchemy."

Celia knew that Rosso was storing this up for later. Her at groin height, looking up at him with wide dark eyes.

You're a long way from home.

"Whatever. I thought you said McNall quit?"

His smirk faltered. "Hm?"

"The blonde lady. Could have sworn I saw her leave just as you came in."

Just like that, the smile was back. "I saw no one."

CELIA PRESENTED her third effort in the best possible light, her temples grinding as she awaited the Maestro's arrival. The need for approval chafed her, but it wasn't her money, and she'd hitched herself to the director's train. To the stars or off a cliff, she'd be right alongside him.

The night before had been restless, her headache never really ceasing. With the crew leaving after midnight, Celia had been left alone in the grand studio, the empty spaces a warren of shadows amongst dead sets.

Unable to sleep, she'd walked the building, traipsing through the haunted hotel's lobby, Karina's bedroom, the crypt. The balcony and colossal protruding tree loomed, the facade of the Queen Anne hotel tottering over the white picket fence, and she studied this most of all, the encroaching forest painted against the far wall, fake trees dotting the yard for perspective.

The gag itself wouldn't be hard, she knew. Once Frazzi had filmed the jump, they'd put the actor on a bicycle seat drilled into the post, supporting their weight while remaining invisible beneath the gown. Celia had already visualized the execution, the camera zooming into the jagged wooden edge, the branches jabbing into the cast and pushing its eyes aside like pesky jelly. Spasming and kicking, the actor would be a three-point ruin as the tiny hoses behind the mask spewed a fountain of scarlet.

Savini of Ohio.

But she'd had the uncomfortable feeling of being watched. Not hokey, as if the dead warlock from the film was still strutting the boards, but rather--something else.

Someone else.

She'd kept imagining blonde hair drifting around corners, wafting at the edges of her vision.

And the eyes.

The first two masks she'd done were garbage. She'd recognized her failure immediately and attributed her error to the earlier photos. Some of them, she swore, were slightly altered, different than the film. There was no personality, the mix of intrigue and vulnerability that made Karina McNall so absorbing, and the frustration had stifled her. They were on a schedule, and needed her to produce. But this--

Celia knew gold when she saw it. A lifelike representation of the face that now haunted her hours.

Nothing could have prepared her for the director's reaction.

Lucio Frazzi bulled into the room. Rosso trailed him like an ill-smelling kite. The maestro spit two words. Her heart sank.

"Who's this?"

Frazzi gestured at the model's orbital sockets, the aquamarine eyes. What he spat at Rosso was a steamrolling train.

"Chin is correct, but the cheekbones need to be higher. And the eyes, all wrong." Rosso paused, ingesting another tirade. "There is no vision here. No spirit. One's eyes are inherited wisdom. All Karina saw imprinted there."

Frazzi swatted the cast from the table, steely hair flying from beneath his cap, and growled. Rosso smirked. "What you have produced is only paint."

Clenching her fists, Celia resisted the urge to raise a photo up to the facial cast. She could see Karina in her mind's eye, hair flowing about her shoulders, welcoming. Reacting. Screaming.

"With all due--"

"Without the eyes, there is nothing. Karina, he has known for years. Known her, with a man's eye for woman." Rosso watched Frazzi storm out of the workspace. "Perhaps that is the problem."

Celia swallowed a dozen curt responses as the go-between disappeared. She followed him out onto the studio floor, where the crew had gathered around an exterior window.

Frazzi leapt into his chair, shouting for action.

Without warning, India was slammed against the breakaway pane by an arm wearing a dark glove. The glove's wearer, a crew member out of the shot, was doing his best to stay awake.

Frazzi shouted, and they did it again. This time, the glass shook with the impact, cracked, then shattered.

The maestro shouted, and the glass was replaced. Again.

And again.

And again.

His own daughter.

CELIA RAN through the rough footage again, then a third time, the reek of cigarette smoke filling the room as the operator downed Moretti after Moretti.

Rather than adjust to the unspooling horrors, though, her unease only grew. With each viewing, she discovered more discrepancies in the shots, odd angles chosen, discordant and mistranslated items in the backgrounds.

Most of all, she absorbed McNall.

The enticing way the actor's head would tilt when introduced, one eyebrow slightly raising. The tiny nod of her chin as punctuation on a scream. The faintest of scars along one cheek-bone, a minuscule white line no more than a centimeter across, adding character and vulnerability to each movement.

But the eyes--

Frazzi was right, damn it.

There was an allure there, a sharp intelligence. A sly humor to her view of the world, with a vulnerability that drew people in. Celia had made sketch after sketch of just the actor's eyes, trying to match them perfectly.

The combination of pupil and iris. The black furrows radiating through the oceanic color, the thin limbal ring that hedged in that palette.

She was closer than she'd ever been.

Emboldened, she began her fourth as the operator called it a day. Taking her time on the subtler details, she tried to weave in all she'd learned. The grinding behind her eyes swelled into thudding agony.

As silly as it sounded, Celia felt she knew Karina.

Intimately, even.

But she hadn't been able to shake the feeling of being watched. Every so often, as she went to the racks to resupply, she thought she spotted the light bob of fair hair, rounding corners in the occulted distance of the set. A pale face, glimpsed in the shadows. The slightest glint of aquamarine, reflected in the workspace lights.

It's your imagination.

No one calls you halfway around the world as a prank.

Karina McNall is not lurking on set.

But she didn't believe it.

Either way, they would still need the FX for the stunt. Why only increase the difficulty in making it?

It would be so good to finally meet her.

Just for reference, of course.

Just to see if you got all the curves right.

Her heart quickened. The warm feeling below her belly was nothing, only homesickness.

When she was finished, the end result almost breathed.

She held it up to her face.

It would be the most natural thing in the world to put it on.

There was a slight scuffle behind her, and Celia dropped the mask to the table, jerking her head around to the illusory shadows.

She thought she saw the door glide shut.

The faintest glimpse of fair hair.

Racing over to the entrance, Celia threw it open. But all there were on set were shadows: the looming Queen Anne and tree a pitched gallows.

"BELLISIMO!"

Well out of the shot, Celia crouched behind the faux bed. The cast of India's gaping, broken mouth she'd refined, and she now pumped gelatinous blood through the gap. When Frazzi gave the word, she began thrusting the entrails through.

Rosso had procured them at the local butcher, and they reeked, on the verge of complete spoilage. The go-between hadn't thought to refrigerate them, only plopping them down in a paper sack at the corner of the workspace.

It was repugnant. It was awful.

And it worked.

Lucio Frazzi shouted, leaping from his chair and strutting onto the set. Traipsing through the gore, he gave her an uncomfortable half-hug and in Italian sang her praises.

At least, that's what she thought he was doing. Rosso had already gone to investigate the mask, so she had no idea if she was being celebrated or damned.

Then Frazzi gestured her back to her workspace.

Just like that, the migraine came thundering back.

For a moment, she had felt like part of the production.

Part of the magic.

The director flung open her door, treading bloody bootprints inside. She followed, a leaf caught in the tailwind of a gory hurricane, and watched him storm over to the heavy worktable at the far end of the room.

Holding them up to the light, he lifted first the mask, then the cast. Rosso perched on the corner stool, a cigarette dangling, thumbing disinterestedly through her sketchpads.

With a shake of his head, the director let her work fall to earth.

McNall's chin shattered, the shards spiraling in a slow doldrum across the concrete floor.

Fury limned her vision in scarlet. She had flown halfway around the world. Given up her day job clerking, dead end though it was, to be here. And to be treated--

Spitting a few sentences at Rosso, Frazzi slumped on the nearby stool, running a hand through his steely hair.

Rosso was unmoved. "The Savini of Ohio, Dario called you. We take a chance. But as time runs out, you fail."

Before she could speak, Rosso pushed on. "The sculpture, adequate. The likeness, exquisite. But the eyes--"

Inexplicably, Frazzi began to sob.

The horrible urge to go to his side and comfort him rose in her.

Celia stomped it to death.

What's wrong with you?

"--they are not Karina's. None of her spirit. None of her heart."

"Bullshit." Unsure which of them to direct it to, Celia glared down a point in the middle. "I've studied every article you've given me. I've been through the photos half a dozen times, watched the footage until that operator was ready to marry me. That's your lead actress. At least, until you fucking broke it."

"No." Rosso lit another cigarette, grinding out the first on the cover of her sketchpad. "Perhaps if you watched--"

The director hissed something at Rosso, staring him down.

Rosso turned back to her. "The maestro is an artist. The sequence, it is incomplete. Not yet."

"The *director*, and I've got my doubts. Unless it's a different movie, I've seen the fucking footage."

"Shut your whoring mouth." Rosso stood, tossing her sketchbook aside, and stepped towards her. The waft of Brut filled the air like a threat of violence, and for a moment she realized just how far from home she really was.

Anything can happen here.

Anything at all.

"We need the mask. The cast. This is how we make the magic happen."

"Who are you kidding?" Celia fought the urge to retreat. "Just bring in McNall."

Rosso froze. Frazzi only stared at her.

"Are you saying she's not here? Come on. I've seen her on set. Hell, in this fucking room."

"No." Rosso recovered, mumbling something to the director. "Impossible."

"It would be so much easier--"

Rosso pushed it aside. "It's not possible."

Frazzi rose, an Atlas crushed beneath the world. He whispered something to Rosso, then headed for the door.

"We left her in Louisiana," the go-between translated, and disappeared.

IN THE END, Celia went back to work.

It was that or quit, and she refused to skulk back to Dayton with nothing.

Worse, she had something to prove.

Celia viewed the rough footage over and over, swatting the operator's hands aside whenever they drifted near. Evidently the repeat exhibitions had led him to believe she wanted to bear his child.

The film crept inside her. With each viewing, she spotted more and more of the discordant touches Lucio had become famous for. Bizarre paintings. Strange writing. Objects in the background that didn't belong. Random side-jabs of dialogue with no relevance or deliberate obfuscations.

It was discomfiting, to say the least. The trancelike, haunted state it infused in her was ghastly, the pounding migraines an astral visitation that shook her to her core.

But, at last, she'd found the flaw.

Brushing aside her failures, Celia started again, setting up the pictures and sketches for reference. As the rejected operator slumped over on his stool, she was aware of someone else in the room, the sensation of eyes upon her.

Good.

Let them see.

She didn't turn, only raced back and forth to the shelves, gathering plaster, paint, brushes, latex.

It had always been there. The slightest dash of heterochromia descending from McNall's right pupil, a thin strip of hazel like an upside-down *t* amongst the aquamarine.

Why didn't you see it sooner?

The answer was simple.

You weren't ready.

The unwelcome thought chimed within her skull, and she tried to clear it, busying her hands and emptying her mind as both the mask and cast gained shape.

After so many tries, it was easy.

She knew it as if it were her own face.

Footsteps closed the distance behind her, light and breathy against the bare floor. Celia paid them no mind.

Time melted. Finally, Celia set down the mask and cast, slipping an exploratory finger into the orbital sockets, plopping out the spectacular eyes with a sideways thrust.

She felt cool breath on the back of her neck, the warmth of another person leaning in close, radiating heat against her skin.

Wisps of blonde hair floated in her periphery.

As she began to turn, she heard a clap.

Then the presence was gone.

"Bellisimo."

TEETERING ON THE FAUX BALCONY, Celia's heart raced, disbelieving, eyes blind.

At least she'd be going back to Dayton with something.

This is how we make the magic happen.

Frazzi had approved the final product without hesitation, all enmity gone. With hurried words and telling glances from Rosso, she'd been praised as a Michelangelo, the likeness she'd created deemed perfect.

Then they sprung the trap.

Without McNall, they had no similar actor.

No one to finish the shots.

And Celia was of a height--

Celia had to point out that she was nowhere near as endowed, but Rosso waved it away as mere costuming. She'd subsequently drawn blood, negotiating her role in the next two productions. *The Thirteenth Chapel. Menagerie of Souls.*

But it should have been obvious.

Someone had to do the stunt.

On paper, it wasn't this live nightmare. Just leap from the balcony, narrowly miss the fence, and slam into the shallow dug-out filled with foam.

Walk away with a career.

Above the bayou, she felt the blonde hair flowing around the mask she wore, the welcoming caress about her shoulders.

The director's vision had been spelled out a dozen times.

Glimpsing the horror, McNall would pivot in terror. Spreading her arms wide, she'd jump.

But with their insistence on making the eyes a part of the mask, Celia couldn't see a thing. That she would trust her life to someone who thought the human skull could be crushed by hand was unimaginable when she'd first boarded the plane to Florence.

Still, here she was.

Karina McNall, her face a perfect likeness.

And about to do what the actor would never.

Her suggestion made flesh, they'd filmed the last part first. Celia had perched on a bicycle seat drilled into the fence, a scarlet swath of gore painted between her legs as she straddled the sawed-off post. The branches were affixed to the front of the mask, the red ruin of the gorgeous eyes only goopy runnels against the construct.

They'd filmed the gore shots next, the cast working flawlessly. The tree punctured the orbitals, pushing the crafted eyes out in a carmine spray. It was strange, seeing her work actualized to this extent, her own face honed to perfection then destroyed in less than five minutes, but by then the cast was only a construct again.

They didn't need it anymore.

They had Karina now.

But the jump--

Celia stood on her mark, the world dark around her. She'd tried it without the mask three times that afternoon, each leap a breathtaking feeling of weightlessness, an untethering that seemed to go on forever as Karina's gown rustled and fluttered before she slammed into the pit of foam.

They could have made the hole bigger, at least. Farther away from the fence post, which admittedly looked pretty fucking jagged from the balcony.

But this was it.

Impossible.

From somewhere below her, Frazzi yelled for action. The world dwindled to a rush of sound and feeling.

Pivot. Three steps.

Boosting herself, the rough wood beneath her fingers.

Spreading her arms, she let Karina fly.

Rosso stopped by her workspace just as Celia was finishing packing her bag.

"The maestro. He needs to see you."

She'd expected as much. Craved it, really, even with the migraine grinding behind her eyes, so much worse since yesterday. Part of her still recoiled from the need, a puppy at the master's leg, but Celia had put so much into the project it was a wonder she was still breathing.

She followed Rosso through the abandoned sets, the stricken stage, the balcony and fencepost where she'd become McNall, if only for a few hours. Their steps were absurdly loud in the empty space, devoid of people, bereft of light.

Rosso led her to a grey door she'd never seen before.

Without a word, he pushed it open.

Frazzi was inside the dim room, a leather chair resting before the projection screen. The go-between crossed the room in silence.

The director fixed her with his one good eye and motioned her to sit, steely hair tucked under his flat cap.

"Do you want to see?"

That the words were in English startled her, and suddenly, she wasn't so sure. It occurred to her that she could simply walk out. Go home. Be the Savini of Ohio.

Maybe that wouldn't be so bad.

But that was crazy.

You made the magic happen.

And you need to see.

Blonde tendrils drifted across her face, obscuring her vision. "What really happened in Louisiana?"

Frazzi only smiled.

The film began.

A discordant jangle of prog-rock, then sweeping synth across the black swamp. Celia felt herself sinking deeper into the chair as she saw her image on screen, the scenes clumsily bleeding into each other. The director wasn't showing her the raw footage.

This was a rough cut of the film itself.

As side characters tottered into parodies of gore, she realized that what Rosso had said was true. There was a grand alchemy to the sequence, each discordant element a component of a spell. It was madness, but a beautiful, bludgeoning insanity. With each new horror crashing waves against her mind, Celia felt herself begin to drift, the thudding pain easing.

She smiled.

There she was, in the lobby of the haunted hotel. Racing with India through the deserted basement of the courthouse. Seeking sanctuary in the nave of the abandoned church.

Without a glance at his work, Frazzi stared only at her, black eyepatch a gaping void. His one good eye winked infernal in the projected light.

The footage was gorgeously abhorrent.

There she was, digging in the old cemetery. In Room 39 as India was butchered across the way. In the crypts beneath the hotel.

A grotesque glory birthing.

There she was, in the hospital morgue as the dead began to swarm. At the old library, burning the book. Back on the balcony, with a convulsive shudder of flight.

She watched herself fly, if only for an instant.

Her body pierced.

Her aquamarine eyes torn from her head.

Then how did she now see?

As the film faded to black, a crash of synth and drums erupted, a maelstrom at the cessation of the world. Then nothing.

"Karina," Lucio breathed.

She slid her hand into his. "Maestro."

I'M THE LAST PERSON I'D WANT TO BE

IRA RAT

"(T)here are things we can't see now, that are there, that are embedded, that it takes time in order to be able to see."

— LYNN HERSHMAN LEESON

WHEN I WAS 7, MY FATHER HIT ME SO HARD IN THE CHEST THAT I FELT my soul leave my body.

Stop doing that, he said.

I still don't know what I had been doing, but I was damn sure never to do anything again.

1973

"Jesus, what a shithole." The apartment is one coat of fresh paint above a skid row flophouse: open kitchen, open bathroom, open window. The word "NoModCons" flashes in my head with a red ballpoint star next to it. Though, looking around, I'm not sure if I see any conveniences, modern or otherwise.

I sure do know how to pick 'em. Over the phone, the landlord had said that I could look the place over before committing to the first month's rent. But given my savings, this was my only option.

Scanning the concrete floor painted a putrid sort of green, it's at least mildly reassuring that there isn't a masking tape outline of a body. At least if there had been one, they were courteous enough to remove the evidence before I got here.

...small favors, I guess.

The earthy smell of mold invades my nose, and I start to think about the abandoned factory I photographed years before. A fire had eaten a hole in the ceiling, and a decade or two of rain had poured in. This place was slightly better than that, and what did I expect for 45 bucks a month? Even if it's Des Moines fucking Iowa.

I'm sure I could have found something cheaper out in the sticks, but living far away from everything without a car would have made the project impossible. The little money I have left should only go towards the essentials and the project itself. Anyway, I've seen much worse.

Bleach, that's step one. Step two, to be determined.

The apartment is roughly what I expected. A counter, a free-standing commode (no door or curtain) that looks like it's been there and never cleaned since the building was constructed sometime in the 1800s, but at least there's enough room to put my stuff. I open the bag containing all my worldly possessions: my Leica, Polaroid, a small mountain of film, a few markers and pens, the last six months of Art in America, a copy of Grapefruit, and three sets of clothes. Even at 150 square feet, there's more than enough space. So, at least I didn't get it in my head that this project needed to be on canvas.

I didn't expect the concrete floor, but it's nothing that a half-dozen blankets from a thrift store won't fix.

A pair of clogs walk past my window. I try to follow the legs up—but she disappears into the mystery of what's beyond my ceiling. I'll also have to buy something to cover that thing up. The idea of people being able to look down here at me whenever they want makes me feel more than a little anxious, and tension works its way up from the bottom of my belly until my fingers start to twitch, like a smoker who ran out when all the stores are closed.

I take out the Polaroid and set it on the counter. Reaching out, I press the shutter; the flash goes off. First, you pull the front tab and then pull out the second to get the picture, I recite to myself. I had picked up the brand new "Big Swinger" just before I left and read the instructions at least a dozen times on the ride here.

I lift the exposure paper and take a look at myself. My hand goes to my hair, or where it used to be. The hair is now in the garbage of some gas station restroom somewhere between there and here. One of many stops the bus took along the way. Next, the hand gingerly goes to my nose. As I look at the bandage across its bridge, it is nearly one huge pitch-black square splotch on the photograph.

It probably needs stitches. That isn't in the budget, either. It's just going to have to wait, or else I'll have to live with the scar. I peel off the bandage and take another picture. This time I can see the edges of the wound across my nose curling up into an Elvis sneer, pulled up to one side. Like a second mouth. I never asked for the first one. The asymmetry bothers me more than the gash itself. I look around the room for a mirror but come up empty.

In the picture, dust in the air catches the reflection of the flash, making white freckles like tiny snowflakes or flowers dapple across the tear in my skin. At least I don't look like me. That's the whole point of moving so far away, to be someone else. Right now, I'm the last person I'd want to be.

SECOND DAY HERE, and I already have a job at a diner. The owner said he didn't have anywhere else to put me than dishwashing until the bandage came off. Wouldn't look right, he said. I don't need people thinking I'm beating up my employees any more than they already do. And then he laughed so hard it sent him into a coughing fit, spit and sweat diffusing into the air like perfume at a cosmetic counter.

My hands jerked reflexively up to my chest. But I didn't say anything.

The less I have to talk to people, the better. I'm still working on my voice, and don't want to spoil any illusions.

I start work right away, and all they play all day is AM radio, saccharine and sweet. It's like the Carpenters and Osmonds started breeding together to take over the airwaves. Like the children from Village of the Damned but backed by the finest studio musicians the record labels have to offer. It could be worse. At least it's not a bunch of hippy shit.

I walk into the seating area after my shift. A man sitting at the end of the counter looks dried and crumbled into himself, his movements puppet-like and stiff.

Things grow down there, he says in a raspy feminine voice. His movements and speech are so slow that they'd be going backward if they could.

What? I ask.

I feel an unwelcome hand on my shoulder, and I nearly collapse. Don't mind him, the owner offers. He's always saying weird shit to people, especially people he's never seen before. It's just nonsense. His voice hushes. He comes here every day, and orders pancakes and coffee, sitting there pecking at his food and getting refills till we close.

THE PROBLEM IS that people spend more time talking than they do listening. I know. I'm guilty of it myself. The impulse to be heard is a potent drug. Most don't have the willpower to resist. And trying to understand anybody or anything outside of yourself is something the vast majority won't even begin to consider.

For example, my professors at Cranbrook have been teaching the same way since before Jackson Pollock was a sperm. You would be hard-pressed to find a few who even thought photography was an art. Anything that didn't resemble a Rembrandt or a Renoir was entirely out of the question.

Something I forgot to ask about while taking the tour of the campus, I guess. I'll chalk it up to my naïveté, as most of them hadn't kept up with art theory past the first World War. The idea that Dali, Rauschenberg, Warhol were their art, and what they produced was just secondary was something that most of them couldn't even wrap their head around, let alone actually teach and support in their students was just out of the question.

After a year of discussing my ideas with them, with a lot of gallery art buzzwords like "identity," "performance art," and "the lucid ephemeral," one of my teachers gave me a check for $200. For materials, getting away, he said. He claimed it was an artist grant he had applied for on my behalf. I didn't doubt that it came out of his pocket.

The next time I saw him, his hand found its way to my knee and started slowly moving up. I don't know if he took my silence as encouragement, but I couldn't have opened my mouth if I tried. Fortunately, someone came into the room, and I fled to the bus station a week early.

I TAKE OUT THE POLAROID, set it on the counter. Reaching out, I press the shutter; the flash goes off. First, you pull the front tab and then pull out the second to get the picture. I lift the exposure paper and look at myself. The wound across the bridge of my nose is even bigger than in the last several shots, the edges spongy like old fruit. I figured, from looking at the stack of pictures, that it wasn't really dappled light or dust. It appears more like new skin starting to form, but that doesn't happen, does it? I should have paid more attention in biology.

Little splotches of white on the raw flesh underneath my skin.

I press the edges together, and rather than an Elvis snarl, I see a Cheshire grin. Alice has nothing on me, or rather that cat doesn't. In a book by Kenneth Anger, I remember reading that Disney would press his erect penis against little boys and girls when they would come and sit in "Uncle Walt's" lap. Maybe, that's when the last bit of my childhood illusions finally died, not that I had many to begin with.

After my father hit me, I never talked to him or my mother again. There was a handful of change sitting on the counter for me every Monday for lunch and other kid expenses. Never enough to last through Friday. We picked up our dinner plates and went to our respective areas every night. We were room-mates. Nothing more.

The money disappeared when mom caught me waiting tables.

When I left for college, I didn't say goodbye.

MY NAME IS GRAY SORENSEN. I repeat to myself, a little higher, a little lower, and then back up a notch.

I'd spent the morning practicing a sob story about losing my ID, but the woman at the Ankeny DMV waved me off. Gray seemed as good as any name. She didn't ask any questions. Didn't even ask for proof. She said I should come back when I don't have the bandage anymore. It was unsightly and would be hard for people checking it to recognize me.

It's not like I need it for anything other than the project. I take the ID home and stick it in an envelope, already busting at the seams with Polaroids. Along with my first month's rent notice.

MY name is Gray Sorensen.

My NAME is Gray Sorensen.

My name IS Gray Sorensen.

You can scrub your life of as many identifiers as you can, but people will always insist on a name.

Every piece of art needs one.

I WAKE up to the sound of my father breathing. I know it can't be him because he's dead, but his unmistakable presence lingers. I go over and turn on the single bulb dangling from the ceiling. There is nothing but the nest of blankets I stole from the donation pile outside a closed Salvation Army. I should feel bad about that, I think. I just don't.

Tears run down my face, but when I wipe them away, my hands are covered in white liquid tinged with a slight pinkness; must be pus from the wound. One month and 100 pictures later, it isn't looking any better. The rotten fruit pucker of its edges is deeply pockmarked. It even droops over the edge of my nose when I take the bandage off.

I take out the Polaroid, set it on the counter. Reaching out, I press the shutter; the flash goes off. First, you pull the front tab and then pull out the second to get the picture. I leave it in the envelope without looking at it.

Been feeling weak. Maybe the gash is making me anemic. Either way, I've been sleeping most of the hours I'm not at the diner. It's slowing down the project, but it should be better soon. I have months before I need to start curating the bits and pieces to see how I'll display this, what fragmented parts still need to be filled. Narrowing down what ritzy galleries I should contact. What galleries represent Warhol? I'll have to check my list later. Might as well start at the top, at least the top of the places I'd want "Gray" to be seen.

But when this comes out, is Gray just the subject or also the creator? Who am I when I start to try to parcel out who gets credit? Or is there a separation at all? After all this, will "Gray" become nothing, or do I?

FRANKENSTEIN STITCHES ARE the best I can do. The flesh sags around the crude, uneven loops of thread.

I picked up a small mirror, needle, and thread from Woolworths. I probably should have gotten something to disinfect it, or at least my face. At this point, I'm not sure it even matters. The smell of fresh soil seeps from my skin. Underneath it, the once raw red meat has nearly turned the color of boiled pork from the hundreds of little splotches knitting together.

You've been hurt a long time. The old man says to me from the other side of the counter in his gravely androgynous voice. I reach to my face, but my hand ends up on my chest. What do you mean? I ask in a thin and wobbly voice that I've never heard come out of my mouth before.

Headlights go by the diner's windows and cast shadows of big fat snowflakes on the walls. A monochromatic light show that nobody asked for, but for a moment, I appreciate the distraction. A moment of reality in what has felt like a bad B-movie ever since I stepped off the bus in this town. A film that I have no conscious control of, though I wrote the script. Alone, in my dorm room, a lifetime ago.

This basement is a meat locker. I feel sick. My body's sore in a way that's worse than any flu I've ever had. Did I come down with something? I see my breath as I cough. My chest feels heavy with congestion. Getting out of these blankets sounds like a hell, but it's time to take another photograph.

I lift the exposure paper and look at myself.

A small flower pokes out from between my uneven stitches, right on the bridge of my nose. A tiny white flower like they use as filler in bouquets. Half-stained pink from the ooze that continues to drip into my bandages every day.

I try to pluck it, but it makes me feel like I'm falling through a void.

I pull at the stitches, and they come out without any effort.

Just the slow, uncomfortable feeling of floss being dragged across my gums. Tender and as deliberate as I can be until they're gone, and the skin falls loose again, now drooping down past my bottom lip.

I press the shutter; the flash goes off.

From the bottom of my vision, I see many of the flowers sprouting from the meat of my face. As if controlled by someone else, my hand goes to the loose skin and I tug. It rips like tissue paper. I keep going, and more flowers grow down my neck.

I press the shutter; the flash goes off. The previous photo falls to the floor, unexposed.

I keep pulling, and the skin is almost completely gone from my head and shoulders. It falls down my back like the hood of a jacket.

I press the shutter; the flash goes off. The previous one falls to the floor.

I pull at my collar, tugging like trying to rip off a shirt, and my skin comes away effortlessly. From the center of my chest, a single red flower springs up like a jack-in-the-box.

I grab the flower by the stem and once again feel faint as it comes loose.

Another picture falls to the floor.

THE DANCER, THE DANCE

DONYAE COLES

THE CANVAS STARED BACK AT YEVA, BLEACHED SKULL WHITE, ITS blankness close enough to a grin to make her stomach churn. Her fingers wrapped tight, forming a fist around the brush hard enough to snap it. The canvas taunted her with its whiteness. Its nothing. (She hadn't slept in days.)

She hadn't painted in just as long.

The two kept step with each other, the insomnia, the failure of her creativity. She tried to break up their dance; she rained her attempts all over the studio floor. Thick, charcoal lines slashed gray newsprint. A figure that spun and refused to form on every page, tossed to the ground. Pages spread like legs and she sat in between them waiting to be birthed, waiting to birth. But the canvas stayed pure. Unmarked. Untouched.

It had to be perfect. None of her sketches had been. None of the thumbnails. None of the trials. She had only the one canvas. She couldn't get another. Couldn't make another. She sighed, stepped back. It wasn't *right*. It wasn't *ready*.

She moved to put down the brush, pick up the charcoal again. Reached for the stack of newsprint. Stopped.

That was the failure. The sunlight made everything hazy. Lack of sleep, lack of dreams, made everything a dream. So close to that sweet fountain she could taste it. It was never meant for paper. She was never meant for paper.

She'd be born on skin, wet and messy. From flesh to flesh.

Yeva dropped the dark stick. Picked up a tube of paint, squeezed a fat blob onto the gray palette. It emerged clay brown. She dipped her brush in, picked up the color and turned to her canvas.

It took up the whole easel. The bottom sat along the shelf at the foot; the top was clamped down with the last inch of the back brace. Tall, taller than her, nearly nine feet. She'd made it herself. Started the project when her sleep started to slip from her.

"Your work is too safe. You need to stand out. I wanna bring you up with me but you're not ready yet," he had said. Ryan, the darling, the star. He ran his thumb under her eye, prodding the bruise left by the night (she hadn't slept in days). A purple-red half ring, the sucking hungry kiss mark of her exhaustion. He looked like he would kiss her, but his phone rang. "Put more of yourself into your work!" And then he was gone.

But she already knew what he thought of her work. That's why she started the project. Linen wouldn't work. She needed something different. Something to stand out. She needed skin.

Hide.

The front was impossibly white, chemically white from the gesso but the back was still natural. She wondered if Ryan had ever done that. Stretched his own canvas. He said she had potential. Found her at a local gallery, invited her out. But still, none of his connections had come to her. She wasn't ready, he said. She shook her head, chased thoughts of him away. This was her work.

Thick gesso applied in layers hid the stitches that created the surface she craved. There hadn't been a large enough skin to create the canvas she needed, one that stretched to the heavens and so she took many. They weren't perfect at first, they were ill matched, the hides, the shape of living things and the colors, dusty rose, rose peach, close but not perfect. But she made it work. Stitched them together, slathered them over with bright white.

The back left messy, real. The wood still rough, she was no carpenter, had only invested in the bare minimum needed to cut the boards, nail them together. She spent her money on the more important tools. An artist knows where to spend and where to save for the best result. The staples, chaotic, clustered over each other but there, holding. The whole thing holding.

(She hadn't slept in days.)

The brush deposited paint on the canvas, destroying its purity with a determined swipe of burnt sienna. Yeva jerked her arm angrily across the surface, leaving harsh marks. Wet and thick at the start. Deep brown lines, the color of rust, the color of something alive left to dry, began to form a shape. Curves that became not a person but a figure, clear as anything. It burned a hole in her retina.

Insomnia settled over her like a lover, keeping her awake in the deep dark of early morning. Get out of bed, do something else the articles said. She did. *She tried.* Let the art take her, make something of her while she stumbled in a haze.

She made the canvas to have something to do. She'd never done it before but she found the information online, bought what she needed from sellers through Craigslist. Overnighted the tools she needed to prepare the hide. She was an *artist.* She knew how important the right tools were. Hauled it all into her studio. Put it together in the deep dark when she couldn't sleep.

The first was a mess. It smelled so bad and she'd ruined the skin. But she had to do it herself. She learned from exploring online. Carried the small animal, her first practice, already dead and drained into her space, her studio. It had been a ballet studio before she rented it and filled it with easels and paint and now this new practice.

Yeva cleared pencils and paper pads from a table and set the first one down. Couldn't bear to think of it as anything but *the skin.* Used her tools to part skin from muscle, buff titanium from peach and cadmium red. Tanned it with its own brains, a brown that leaned towards grey. She dumped the meat in the garbage. The meat was waste, she couldn't paint on it. She just needed the skin. Upstairs her neighbors played music that thumped through the floor.

That first skin was there, all torn imperfect pieces, stitched along with the others. It was part of her canvas.

Yeva frowned, pulling her brush into a wide arc. A sweeping arm topped with slashed lines that would be fingers. A ghost of color from the nearly depleted bristles. All of it poised above a blank oval that would be a face. Would be something. As she would be something, someday. Ryan was wrong about her. She was ready. She bit at the inside of her mouth, brush floating in the air.

Was this enough?

The art called her, dragged her back to the canvas away from the doubts. The Dancer that wanted to be. The drive to create crawled along her arms, up her back and over her skull like ants. Yeva moved to brush them off. Her fingers met bandages. Chemical white. Couldn't bear to think about them. She dropped her hands, searched with her eyes until she found a stool. Dragged it over and climbed up to reach the highest parts of the canvas, to lay down the rest of the scene.

She had tried to paint trial pieces. There was only the one canvas, she had to get it right. She had meant to make a collection, a series. That was Ryan's advice. "Next time you feel something, a mood, do ten paintings about it. Instant show," he said over one of their "mentoring sessions". Yeva tried, it wasn't good enough. Those canvases sat stacked against the wall, pedestrian. She needed to try again with the Dancer. Started small to get the motion, the color down. Slashes of paint. Clouds of ochre. Alzarin ground. And the Dancer. Faceless motion. Each one too small, not worth finishing. She moved to the next size and then again until a stack of canvases, half painted with the gesture of the dance, each one the form closer, more realized but not right. Because those canvases were linen and duck cloth and the Dancer needed flesh. Demanded it.

Nothing else would reveal the Dancer.

The next one was bigger and Yeva saved more of that skin. The one after that near perfect. It didn't take much to learn, not when you had an eye, not when you practiced the motions before making the first mark. These went into the piece too. How long had it been since she'd seen Ryan? How long had it been since she slept? (She hadn't slept in days.)

No answers but there was the canvas. Finished and beautiful and *unique*. Just as Ryan had advised her.

Yeva mixed white and black into the rust creating tones, setting a scene haphazardly as an under painting and sighed as the warm rush of *right* flooded her for the first time since the drive had started. Proof that the work she had already put into *this* canvas made it worthy. That she was worthy. (She hadn't slept in days.)

The room closed in on her, dark flashes spun at the edges of her vision. Like wings, the afterimage of a flash, the air when you've had too much to drink. But Yeva painted, quick and bold. Heat rushed through her, her arm felt light, moved fast and free. Excitement, giddiness, the joy! Her cheeks ached as she smiled but she smiled still. This painting would mean something. This painting would *be* something. And then she would be something.

Brush gripped in one hand, smearing blood-rust paint over her skirts before she stopped, eyes locked on the half-realized piece before her. The movement was there, a map of lines, but it lacked some core part. Some key. Yeva wasn't sure what, she had never gotten this far with it. The art had never whispered *right* to her before. (She hadn't slept in days.) *Something was missing.*

She had gotten that way with the canvas too. She had prepared so many pieces. So many different types of skin. Gotten good, took them whole, used every part. Yeva brought them to her studio live, the skins. Made a space for them. Splashed the plastic floor with perylene maroon. The upstairs neighbors played music so loud it came through the ceiling but it didn't matter, she killed quick as silver. Butchered, if it could be called that, the meat, dumped outside the city for the vultures in heavy duty bags.

Hard work but it didn't let her sleep (*she hadn't slept in days*).

Yeva wasn't a butcher. She was an artist but had learned well enough, anything can be learned if you practice. Could probably make more canvases if she wanted but no, this would be the only one. This one had the most important piece. The piece that fit it all together, that whispered *right*.

All gesture, frenzied movement against an alien background.

She held out a hand to them, brown to orange, flesh and blood to flesh and paint and her smile broke open into laughter. A wide grin, all toothy because, yes, *yes,* she saw the next step.

The studio will have a Dancer again, she thought. In that mass of brown leaning towards grey that lived behind her eyes beneath the buzzing and flashing that drove her to paint, she had the idea that perhaps she was channeling the spirit of the dancers that once were, capturing their essence on canvas. She liked the poetry of it. She stepped lightly over to the back wall and tugged the heavy curtains that blocked the mirrors and saw herself staring back. *She hadn't slept in days.*

It wouldn't let her. She understood that now. Yeva had gotten far enough with it, close enough to it to see that. Had to get it out before she could rest. Had to pour that greatness onto the surface. That Ryan had been right. She wasn't ready before but now—now was different.

She looked at herself. *She hadn't slept in days,* not since she stitched up the last of the canvas, buried her eyes in sketches and failed attempts. And before that sleep had come less and less, the soft webs of dreams falling away more and more until there was only her and the skin, a canvas now and she would make it more again.

Messy, black curls half pulled into a bun and piled on top of her head. Her eyes were two bloodshot, brown orbs that stared through bandages at her tawny colored face. The skin a little more yellow than usual but fine, it didn't matter. Her lips had never hid her snaggle tooth, broken as a child, and couldn't do it now but it didn't matter.

Below that, her body waited, covered in a loose t-shirt and a skirt. A moment's hesitation and she cast these off, tossing them into a pile until she stood bare in front of her reflection, taking in the deep fawn colored rolls of her body. The sepia points of her nipples. The midnight that settled between her thighs. She needed a model for the painting.

There is no art like that from life and the only life available was her own. Those animals she had hauled in were gone. Their blood spilled, their hides stretched. Just her now. They wouldn't have been any good anyway, they weren't right. She was right. Her neighbor turned on their music, the beat traveled through the ceiling. She walked back to the canvas, picked up the brush.

Yeva could see it all now. The messy back, her face staring back at her, her body, the Dancer.

She frowned at herself but forced her eyes to turn back to the gesture on the canvas. She swung back to the mirror, drawing her arm above her head, twisting her body, mimicking the pose.

Her red-veined eyes darted, holding the image in her (not) grey matter before she dropped her hands and dashed back to her palette.

Naked she mixed colors quickly. Crimson speared with sap green and a drop of phthalo blue, she struck the canvas. Quick brush strokes until there was a body. A head, a neck, breasts, belly and then lower, lower, lower, her own flesh and blood belly pressed to the floor to get the first layer down for the foot.

Through the ceiling she heard music. Just the bass, thumping down to her. She didn't know the song but hummed anyway. She had gotten good with her tools, with the flesh, but it was never like this, never the same as the paint. This, this was her talent. Her real skill. Her real self.

No good, she thought and struck the pose again. Her gaze this time directly on her own flesh, not a reflection but on herself. She could see how the light moved against her, sunset red, against the skin of the canvas. The air hummed and crackled. *Yes, yes,* she thought, excited as she painted. There, the arm long, the fingers alien almost but oh so graceful. Was that really her arm? She had never noticed but she swept the paint over the canvas, forming the Dancer. Trusting her body to know. Trusting her eye.

Then the hips and Yeva looked down at the curve of herself moving in time with that distant music. *Paint what you see,* she reminded her hand, *not what you think you see.* She made her thighs thick, her stomach the pouch she stared down at under heavy, round breasts. Not how she wished she would appear, no she painted what her mind understood from what her eyes captured.

It had to be right. That feeling, no, the sound she realized, the soft whisper of the painting said that it was *right,* that she was painting it *true.*

She hadn't slept in days.

The canvas didn't matter anymore because finally, finally Yeva was *painting.* Diving, spinning, reveling in it. The canvas the door, the gate and she had burst it open, spilling over onto the other side birthed in a sea of thick, wet color.

She didn't look at any part of herself twice. She painted quickly, boldly. It was her style. Ryan laughed at it, called it amateur but he didn't understand. He couldn't see. She would make sure he saw. She posed, painted, glazing cobalt to make shadows then more yellow until she, the she on the canvas, the Dancer, seemed to glow in her unfinished world.

She laid down a sky in dioxazine purple, quinacridone violet, and nickel azo yellow blended into something violent, the earth to match, like the bruises from around her eyes. All dark anger, where she was light, light as the Dancer. A temple formed around her, the ceiling ripped away, rubble at her feet all rendered in shadow. Unimportant. Only the figure was important and the figure needed a face.

Memory would serve. Her own face would serve.

She stared with her eyes, windows to her soul. Lovingly she placed them on the canvas, reproducing the whites in a pale blue, threading them with thin red lines of sleeplessness, weighing them down with the bruised lower lids to match the landscape. "She must have been dancing for ages, she's so tired," Yeva mused, sing-song. Then the nose, upturned. The dancer's mouth hung half open in ecstasy and right there: Yeva's snaggle tooth. Broken as a child, never fixed.

Nothing left but her hair. She painted the pile, anthraquinone blue stirred with cadmium orange to make a dark storm of curls. The unruly twists followed the flow of the Dancer on the canvas. The Dancer painted as perfect as she could make it. The Dancer painted to be her.

Smiling, sighing, her eyes wide with delight she stepped back and looked at herself. Her arms held high, her body displayed in plain image against the backdrop of an ancient temple. The name of it whispered in song through the ceiling. She would write it down later but for now she took in what she had created.

She had made the flesh wet again, all those dry, stitched together bits. They had become something more.

The canvas had been right, something about it made the art stronger, more bold. The colors, the depth, it was all so much more. The sun was setting but the painting, her painting, shone brilliant and bright in the coming darkness.

Posing once more to match the painting and a warmth settled over her. *Yes,* it said, *this is good, this is done.* She spun in joy, her greatest work. *She hadn't slept in days.*

Covered in paint and nothing else she turned and saw in that great mirror what she had done.

"Yeva!" Ryan called from the door bursting in without knocking. "I've been trying to get a hold of you! We're supposed to go to an event tonight are you even - whoa!"

She didn't turn, could see him in the mirror, how he stopped, stared at the painting. Her painting.

"This is really, this is, wow." Breathless, awed. No less than she deserved.

She smiled, pain shooting through her but it was all right. Art was pain.

"Oh wow, why are you naked? Yeva?"

She watched him come closer. Crossing the room in long strides.

"My god! What happened to your face girl?" He wrapped his hand around her shoulder, moved to turn her but she stopped him. "Did someone hurt you? Why didn't you call me?"

She turned then, smiled wide, showing off her broken tooth and pointed at the canvas. "It's fine Ryan. My best work."

But he wasn't listening. He could see her face now. The perfect piece to finish her surface.

The eyes and mouth stitched shut, she couldn't have holes in the canvas. And all around it the sheep and pig skin stitched into a rectangle, stapled to the bars that held it. Under the dancer you couldn't see it but there, from behind, in the mirror reflection, it was clear.

Everything that Yeva had put into it.

She had given her all to the painting and it had eaten all, wet and hungry but finished now.

The drums from above played louder and Yeva hummed along, swaying. Ryan was talking, babbling, and calling someone but there were just the drums. The hard pound of the Dancer's feet. She could hear it now. She had reached the precipice. Transformed.

She hadn't slept in days but still she danced.

IN THRALL TO YOUR CATHODE STAR

MATT NEIL HILL

THE COLORS ARE ALL GONE AND THERE IS NOTHING LEFT. CATHODE-RAY flicker in this high-rise concrete cave system the only illumination. Your face, whoever you are. A transmission from the other side of the world, or next door—how can I know? Paralyzed and dying forever, I watch you in the dark. The monochrome glow from ancient screens, battery relays with an acid stink I taste in my sinuses, my teeth; dragged from streets and basements in a past life barely passed, your face the light of my existence. Every wall painted with your cipher; painted with the ashes of the burned world, scooped in calloused handfuls and smeared across cracked plaster, mixed with my black blood and the cancerous rain that still oozes from the sky.

Who films you, I don't know. What your name is, I don't know. Why me, a mystery. I am not the last one. I hear them sometimes: searching, scrabbling, cat-calling the traces of your glow that escape through the boarded windows, the black-out drapes. I turn off the old monitors as they screech, never knowing if there will be enough power to turn them back on. When that day comes, I will navigate these rooms by the *impasto* crests and barbs of your likenesses—your eyelashes, the slack curve of your lips, the vein in your slender throat that pulses far too seldomly for you to ever wake—my shaking hands leading me in circles through this mausoleum, leading me, maze-like, to nowhere.

I thought at first this was a hospital—the piles of burned-out machinery, the bloodied, half-inside out latex gloves and the specter of disinfectant fragrance in the paint and linoleum—but soon it appeared more like an asylum, and then again a prison, and finally, enduringly, like a hybrid of all those places. Melted and melded from concrete, glass, and steel, fire doors scorched of their paint, black monoliths in the dark, forbidding and enticing all at once. A place of twisting corridors and lonely cells of sickness or incarceration that one might leave, but of course might also never.

I have known these institutions, have come and gone.

No unbarred exit has been revealed in recent days, and I have chosen to take this as an omen that I have all I need here for the duration of my life. Afraid to attract others with noise, afraid I might not find my way back if I *were* to exit, this place is now my home. I drink the same water that dilutes the ashes and survive by eating—what might I eat here after all? I turn my back on your image when I eat. I know you would not judge me, but—*but.*

There were so many times in my life before I failed to sell my work; been shunned, wept hungry. But now I would not sell these pieces even if there were anyone left to buy them, not if they wished to pay in bread and apples and clean water. Locked away, they are not for the eyes of others. Creator, curator, custodian, consumer: I am all these, all at once, alone.

Tonight, a close-up of your mouth.

So intimate I imagine I can see the veins beneath, the glacial flow of your life's blood. A dark grey bow, unsmiling. I project your resignation to your fate upon them. I would be swallowed by that mouth, were those lips to part. Static burns a momentary line across them, or perhaps—and I have pondered this before, but chosen not to believe you are not alive, that this is not *live*—a point of damage on a tape rewound and played too often to remain intact. I feel it; the caustic touch of jealousy, that someone else has not only watched you, but had the power over *how* they watched you. I know, rationally, that you are being filmed, that this power exists. Rationality has nothing to do with the acid in my stomach, the bile in my heart.

I must create your mouth anew.

I pile the ashes and drag the old paint and food cans filled with water. My hands, unclean and invisible in the dark, are lit up in the screen's glow. All lines of prophecy obliterated by my work, I am freed from the tyranny of the stars. I mix the shades I need, or as close as I can manage. I struggle to imagine you ever finding these rooms and passing through them, pausing as you recognize these most personal parts of yourself dissected and writ large— or rather when I *have* imagined it, I curl in upon myself in shame; in shame's larger, more aggressive twin, mortification. I would cower in the farthest, darkest corner for fear you see the eyes that stared so hungrily upon you, or the hands that so imperfectly rendered your likeness.

I clear the room's floor. Sliding the monitor gently into the doorway, afraid at every moment that the cables will snag and tear, will disconnect, every scratch and scrape a cacophony that threatens to bring the world down around my ears. But this will be the room; the room that will bear the imprint of your lips on every inch, reverse Sistine never to be beyond my reach. Bare concrete and dirt, crumbs of civilization beneath my sopping palms; threads of my blood swirled through the absence of color to infuse a glimmer of life. I will lay here on future days, if the future arrives, and rest my cheek against your continued silence. I will slow my heart and breath and wait for you to whisper, knowing whatever I hear will be my own invention; not caring.

I reinvent you all the time.

The films change.

Whether the sign of a different hand and eye behind the camera or an inevitable progression, I can't be sure.

I wonder if they know I am watching. I wonder if they know *anyone* is watching. I wonder if whoever filmed this still lives, guerrilla projectionist of the end times.

The films become more intimate yet never reveal who you are.

Your androgyny is amplified beneath the new harshness of the lights. It grows harder for me to transcribe your likeness, no materials available to me pale enough for this new overexposure. I smear great swathes of black across the walls, the negative of you. Tiny whorls rubbed away: your pores, the piercing jut of your hipbones beneath elastic skin stretched to near rupture. None of it satisfies. None of it feels worthy.

Frustrated, I return to the screens, burning my eyes out in the darkness. What I'm shown toys with me, teases me with the unpaintable topography of your skin. The camera swoops in close: medical; a soft bleached forest of down I become lost in. No trail, no way back. So close now I can't know if the image is static or moving. The white grain of heavenly nothing.

And then a jump in the edit; sudden, brutal. Two pairs of hands implying the existence of a third. Black latex fingers, surprisingly gentle, reveal and pull apart your teeth. Hold your mouth open while the second assailant places a plastic apparatus inside to *keep* it open. You make no protest. Obscene, sex doll orifice. My body recoils at the invasiveness of the procedure, but my eyes will not be torn away. Your tongue glistens in its transparent cage. The hands withdraw, then reappear holding a rubber tube slick with lubrication. The black fingers feed it down into the darkness.

The screen goes black, decays into static.

I wait.

Nothing.

For a very long time, nothing.

I HAVE STRUGGLED, for days now I think, to not go out of my mind. Nothing on the screens but the useless reflection of the power light. Static or darkness depending on my mood, on the whims of direct current. I began so many times to paint this new version of you; this screaming marionette, this *ingester:* uncomfortable in my skin at the thought of recreating that passive, involuntary gateway to your viscera. I revisited the mouth room and found I could not stay. Each time my eyes closed I saw that void with its teeth bared and the unheard rush of stale air disappearing into the darkness. All it took was unknown hands clogging your mouth with a plastic *O* to destroy the beautiful purity of those lips. I can no longer see them the same way, loathe myself as a pathetic prude. You did not create that indecent display, and yet it has changed how I view you forever.

When I sleep, I dream of your mouth. In those few washed-out minutes and hours I crawl between your teeth. The scream-echoed portal to a carnival ride that will make me sick, will frighten me. Dark and wet, impossible to turn back from. Sometimes I turn as I pass the flesh and enamel threshold and see the shadow of myself against the wall. Sometimes the black rubber hands are there, their owners in silhouette as the light from their camera shrinks my pupils down to microscopic black stars. Independent of your consciousness, your body's peristalsis inexorably pulls me down and down and down. I wake each time as I am swallowed whole, sometimes the words *help me* in my ears. Sometimes I think what I heard was *this is not for you,* sometimes *you could turn away;* I second guess myself in every waking hour, eyes across my shoulder in the unquiet dark.

And then the screens spark back to life and the awe sticks in my throat.

MY BRAIN FILLS with the absence of color.

Meat, elastic and engorged.

Your inner workings: slow motion fiber-optic crawl. Pulsation and the yield to the camera's progress rules here where the near-dead stillness of your skin did before. Everything is tubes and globes and alien landscapes, the wet horror of us all. You are humanized again. Still my muse, but down from your pedestal to surround me. I blush in the glow of your digestive tract; berate myself for my squeamishness before. I whisper my apologies to the slow on-screen journey through your body. I know you cannot hear me, but—

I have no medical training, but I have seen things; seen things when TV showed more than these phantom transmissions. The dreams of ghosts clawing up from the dirt, their disassembled bones beneath the fractured concrete. There is a sickness in your organs, pockets of disease in black nodes. Unless some new strain of evolution, some burgeoning godhead, but—*no*. You are, if not *dying* inside, then heading *towards* death. *I* am heading towards death, but I had never thought that of you. In your washed-out brilliance I assumed you had achieved some kind of stasis in this broken world, some kind of immortality. The hospital bed your coffin of glass. But now you are the poison apple that rots from within, seemingly perfect until the last.

I have trawled far gutted rooms and swept the ashes into piles. Your inner space adorns the walls: sweet cancerous monuments turned sideways along corridors, spirals of blackest decay exploding from weeping tunnels of flesh. My passion renewed by a sense of battling against time itself. My fingerprints are swollen and distorted by the sheer volume of paint required; no unique signature adorns these works. I don't so much forget to sleep as become incapable. There is simply too much work to be done.

The screens flaunt their metastasizing blossoms, on and on. The motion of the camera slows and stalls. Retraction and progression in a loop, organic malfunction at every turn. My mind takes surreal tangents: the city outside composed of this inner flesh, its crumbling, capsized towers your disease; the impossibility of the contrast between your surface and what roils beneath, the purity and the putrescence; what shines in the light and what festers in the dark. I reside in all these places, subject to their whims. Am *consumed* by them.

The howls outside continue but grow distant, their interest lost. Barbarians unable to break through, beneath me in every sense. Untouchable in my tower of ash. Yet I wake from nightmares of my murals defiled by the offal dragged from my yawning wounds, the echoed whoops of their frenzied destruction. I cry in the dark and quietly check doors I know to be sealed.

The rain still falls, blacker each day. It begins to burn, just the tiniest bit. My thirst is the opposite of quenched, and fingerprints begin to slough away. The barbarians are not required at this point in our extinction event.

Renewed as non-entity, I paint. No one will remember, or even see. A closed gallery at the end of time.

I fail to make connections, and so the connections are made for me.

Please don't, I cry as the scalpel opens the veil between your two realities.

Please, don't, I whisper as the trickle of black blood becomes a flood.

Please stop, I scream as the layers of you are pinned and excised.

THE RETURN of the harsh lights—the *operating theater* lights—has me shielding my eyes: infant cave-dweller's first glimpse of the sun. Impossibly bright, the scalpel blade absorbing and magnifying; a shard of exploding star burning through layers of skin and fat and muscle. The sluice of your cancerous blood washing things black in the black and white. The camera never wavers. The black hands move in and out of frame, methodical and shimmering, fingers clutching gobbets of tumorous flesh. Steel bowls filled to overflowing replaced as an afterthought. There is precision in the work of the blade, yet I still cannot believe any of these unseen forms are surgeons. In my gut this is performance art, reducing me to the role of reporter, of critic.

I cannot tear myself away. I fear what may happen if I do— that the transmission will end; that the gloves will be peeled away and discarded in resignation, the ratio of diseased to healthy tissue too imbalanced. On my knees, my hands tighten into claws, paint drying, unwatched. I wrestle with my desire to immortalize this. I take in the details of your cross-sectioned body; the diminishing number of leaking, uncauterized blood vessels. The grain of the film an echo of your sickness. I am watching either the dismantling or salvation of another human being and my urge is to smear the walls with bodily fluids and the burnt leavings of a broken world rather than to keep vigil. But— that *is* my vigil. If the film ends, if the power dies, my work will be the only memorial to your life, to mine. A grand, brutal descent into extinction marked only by my hands.

With no one left to see.

Futility dragging purpose down into the tar pit.

The hands on screen cut and burn, cut and burn, stopping only when there is nothing left to do of either.

I watch dumbly as the suturing begins. An ocean of breath leaves me. A thousand tiny black *X's* gathering your fault lines together, repair and ruination in each pass of the curved needle. Those black-clad hands so gentle in their found rhythm, an intimacy I could never hope to achieve. Yet strive for all the same, optimistically hopeless. The camera pulls away and we wait, those non-surgeons and I. Like the *bas-relief* atop a mausoleum casket your body fades into the theater table, almost like you were never there at all.

I PAINT and paint and paint.

In the higher rooms least touched by fire I mark great swathes of black across walls a score of shades away from the hue of your skin. The places where you were opened; the places where you were cinched shut. Surgical twine blown up to hold the cracks in the plaster together; illusion of security. What decay still lurks within?

Dimmest light trickles through the cracks in the window boards, enough to work by. I am now as hollowed out as you.

Eating even filth is a memory. A festering shadow creeping through the twilight to leave its mark. Behind and below the batteries die. Up and down the endless stairs: one screen only at the end of the circuit, placed in the room filled with your sleeping mouth. The flex of your ribcage, black mask of ventilator obscuring your face these days. *These* days? You could have been dead for a hundred years. I have searched this endless building, and you are not here, not even your bones. *I know, I know*—but I feel I would know your bones after all this time, is that not clear? Is that not somehow *possible?*

All that matters is that somewhere in time you breathe.

One day the ashes will run out and I will be forced to stop creating or go outside through portals of broken glass. Either would feel like death. Either would *be* death.

I orbit the cathode image of you now like a dead satellite, entropy dragging me slowly down into the last of your light. Elliptical, I shuffle and crawl through the rooms of our shared past, the trajectory of perhaps the final parts of both our lives. The majesty is gone it seems, but there are still times when my dry eyes want to cry. Still times when my sluggish heart becomes arrhythmic. Still times when my cracked lips smile.

One day the last of the batteries will give up the ghost and the screen will go black, and I will never know what became of you. Will you rot on that bed, lungs inflated and deflated by machines even as they liquefy? Will the electricity that runs the apparatus die, and you in turn? Will you still breathe beyond the life of machines? Will you rise—stitched, eviscerated Lazarus—into a bright white afterlife and wonder why you can't remember what you dreamed? Or perhaps wonder at the dreams you *do* remember: the hands black with latex and dripping paint, circling you near and far, keeping you alive on one plane or another.

Or one day—soon, perhaps, it feels, the taste of my own rot on my tongue—my light will go out before that final screen, and it will be your image left alone in the darkness. Time and gravity frozen, and *you* watching over *me.* My bones and rags to keep you company through eternity—be kept company *by* you—both stained with all the work I'd done, and still had yet to do. A curled body bathed in dying light, eyes not quite closed, unable even in my final moments to willingly abandon your image. Lips parted for the world's expiration, both yours and mine. Embracing at the center of a lost maze, a puzzle no one will ever solve. A puzzle no one cares about but that meant everything to me, here at the end of things.

I watch you breathe.

The screen fades.

I wait for you to return.

Just for a while.

In this last darkness.

REGULAR MAINTENANCE OF THE ANXIETY MACHINE

BRENDAN VIDITO

I

My latest medium—pale canvas stretched taut over red, wet clay—lies alone in the fetal position on her couch, a masterwork waiting to be born. Honing my substance to a point, I slice through the veil. The space around me ripples and shimmers in a revolving prism of color. Sliding through, I abscond the void and emerge—disoriented— into the four-dimensional plain where my medium resides. As she slumbers, ignorant to my presence, I begin to work, to paint, to sculpt —to minister the birth of my vision.

Curled up on the couch, Kristina Cameron dreamed of a hallway. Her bare feet tread its length, over mismatched rugs and polished hardwood. One wall was paneled oak. The other dressed with heavy curtains the color of a fine merlot. Behind them, she knew —as one knows in a dream—were a series of raised bedchambers. Each was furnished with a mattress cluttered with pillows, an oil lamp, and a tray of aphrodisiacal incense. The place reminded her of a boutique hotel she had visited with her ex-wife, Gale, on their honeymoon seven years ago. As she wandered, running her fingers along the fabric of the curtains, she mused whether the dream would veer into erotic—her sex life with Gale, unlike virtually every other aspect of their relationship, had been electric. But as she reached the end of the hallway, a chill of unease seized her, erasing all thoughts of arousal.

She was being watched.

Another step and everything changed. She could not shake the feeling that her dream had been hijacked. She now lay naked on a black marble slab. And though her hands and feet were not visibly restrained, she was unable to move. She could not even blink. Water droplets fell in a calculated rhythm from the darkness overhead, landing with lubricating relief on her wide, staring eyes. Directly within her line of sight, but unseen in the darkness, Kristina sensed something huge and imposing looming over the slab. It watched her. Studied her. Dissected her. She could feel the pressure of its gaze on her skin, in the wrinkles of her brain. Oddly, she was not frightened. Rather, she observed these details with a kind of curious awe, tempered only by that whisper of dread.

A second presence, or more accurately, *presences* made themselves known in her peripheral vision—a ring of restless motion encircling the slab. When she focused—she had to squint because she was not wearing her glasses—she saw that it was formed of what appeared to be living busts. Their heads blended seamlessly into elongated shoulders. They were dark and smooth as polished stone. Each possessed a set of glowing, iridescent eyes, and the center of their masses opened in a crooked orifice that leaked, bubbled, and spurted some dark, viscous substance. They watched her intently, an atmosphere of anticipation crackling in the vacuous space around them.

They stirred as something moved, unseen, in the void above Kristina's paralyzed form. She sensed hands kneading the flesh of her stomach, and looked down. The skin dimpled under these invisible ministrations. Pressure increased near her navel—eliciting neither pain nor discomfort—until a concave hollow had formed—a bowl of strained, whitened flesh several inches deep. Abruptly, the skin snapped firm again and Kristina felt those invisible fingers inside her, rearranging, inspecting, prodding, massaging. It was almost as though the thing was shaping a sculpture and her innards were the clay.

A loud knocking resounded in the chamber. It echoed and the living busts blinked their confusion. The hands stopped moving inside her and retreated. The knocking came again—louder this time and more insistent. The chamber started to unravel, grow soft, hazy around the edges and Kristina—

—LURCHED INTO A SITTING POSITION. Drunk with sleep, she glanced around the room, unsure where she was. Cream-colored walls. A photograph of Barb, the old family dog, above the gutted fire-place. Home. Thank god. She was on the couch in her living room, unshowered, and wearing the same sweats as the previous three days. Judging by the dust on the unlit ceiling light, the power was still out. How long had it been now? A week? She couldn't remember. Time had become a meaningless concept.

Someone knocked on her door. She startled at the sound, recalling, however vaguely, the content of her dream: glowing eyes in the dark, the pressure of fingers inside her body—the knocking. She groaned to her feet, sniffed, and rubbed her eyes on her sleeve. Her heart beat its tremulous rhythm, as it always did when she was confronted with the prospect of social interaction —especially now, with the world plunged into darkness.

Warily, Kristina strode toward the entrance. No one was visible through the beveled glass window to the left of the frame. She angled her body so that she was nearly pressed against the door, one ear suspended inches from the cold metal. A neighbor? Unlikely. Her closest neighbor lived over a mile away. This was wine country, after all. Miles of rolling hills sparsely furred with woodlands and veined by tributaries. During the off-season the roads and countryside were eerily calm—even more so now with the blackout.

"Who is it?" she said, loud enough to be heard.

"Police. Open the door."

She frowned. What the hell did the cops want? Did it have something to do with the power? She had heard on the car radio that looting and vandalism were rapidly becoming common occurrences. Perhaps the police were ensuring she was okay?

The man who confronted her when she opened the door—only so far as the security chain would allow—did not look like a police officer. Short but wide, with a square head and small pig-like eyes, he looked more like a caricature than an actual person. Ill-fitting clothes hung in an odd silhouette about his frame, rounded shoulders stretched tight against harsh, unnatural angles. He stank of stale sweat under an eye-watering overlay of deodorant and aftershave. There was something else too, another smell she could not identify. It was at turns cloying and sulfurous, like roses and rotten eggs. His mouth convulsed, lips twitching away from teeth in an unsettling parody of a smile. It reminded Kristina of blood-bloated maggots wriggling away from the bones of a recent meal.

He made a bizarre hand waving gesture, like he was tracing a figure in the air and said, "I am here about the power. May I come in?"

"The power?" Kristina said, taken aback. She felt exposed. Like he was reading her mind. "Why do you need to come in? Can I see some identification, please?"

The man reached into his jacket, produced a leather wallet, and flashed something silver and gleaming in her direction. She blinked and it was gone. She was not even sure what a police badge looked like, not exactly, and the man probably knew this, which explained the rapid, almost dismissive display of his credentials. *Fine*, she thought, even though a shiver of apprehension nagged her. *Let's get this over with.*

Her heartbeat quickened as she unlatched the door, her anxiety rearing its ugly head. She invited the little man inside, stumbling over her words: "I'm in the middle of something, so—unfortunately—I can't host you for long. Ten minutes. Is that cool?"

He looked her up and down and his lips quivered again in a smile. "That is fine."

"Would you like something to drink? I'd offer coffee, but I have no way to boil the water."

"I am fine," the man said and took a seat on the couch, his rear—Kristina noted with a twinge—sinking into the pillows where her head had rested only minutes before.

Kristina lowered into the old rocking chair opposite. The joints creaked under her weight. She rocked nervously. "So, what is this about?" she asked.

The man was looking around the room. Still smiling. "The power," he said.

"What about the power?"

"We did not anticipate such a prolonged absence."

"And what does that have to do with me?"

He stopped looking around the room, his gaze settling on Kristina. "There was a surge from your location," he checked his watch. "Five minutes, thirty-two seconds ago."

"I'm sorry, you lost me."

The man shifted. Placed his hands on his knees and smiled up at the ceiling. "There is more than one party interested in your material, Kristina Cameron."

"My material? What are you talking about?"

The man reached into his jacket pocket. His pale hand emerged clutching an L-shaped object the size of a disposable razor. He pointed it in her direction. His finger twitched—pulling a trigger, she realized too late—and she dropped to the floor, every muscle in her body contracting like a fist. Her bladder released a warm rush down her thighs. Limbs seizing, she tasted blood as her teeth bit deep into her lower lip.

Kristina had never experience real terror until that moment. It expanded to bursting in the pit of her stomach and clawed up her throat, strangling her. Unable to move, powerless, she watched as the man reached again into his jacket pocket and dragged out a rusted hammer. He said, "This is a great honor. Not many have had the privilege to be remade by my hand. My technique will certainly elude you, but I believe one of your cultures employs a similar practice. *Kintsugi*: the art of mending pottery with veins of gold and silver. However, there is an inconsistency in that comparison. *You* are not broken. Not yet."

He raised the hammer and brought it down on her head. A two-inch gash sputtered blood into her eyes. She tried to scream, but only managed a strangled, gurgling croak. Her eyes fluttered. The pain was cataclysmic, an icy, throbbing ache capable of devouring worlds, entire realities. Bile stung the back of her throat.

He dropped his weapon with a brutal thud next to her head. Reaching up, he gripped his upper jaw in both hands—thumbs pressed inside his mouth, behind the front teeth—and before Kristina could puzzle through the pain as to what he was doing, the man started to pull. His upper jaw came away with a sound like someone ripping a wet rag. He gagged as his jaw came away, dragging with it a glistening tubular structure studded with holes.

This is not real. This is not real. Oh Jesus, this can't be real.

Kristina found she could now move her limbs, but terror held her prone. The tubular structure contracted, and an amber fluid suppurated from the holes. The man leaned forward so that his disassembled face hung directly over Kristina's shocked visage. A single drop fell, and as she followed it with her eyes, it visibly corrected its trajectory—as though sentient—and landed with a hiss inside the wound on her scalp.

Kristina screamed. Pain, horror, and confusion vied for dominance inside her mind. She wanted to believe this was nothing but a mental break—a hallucination, a waking nightmare. Anything but the impossible reality staring her in the face. Had she forgotten to take her medication when the blackout started? Was she having another episode? There had been no warning signs. The symptoms could not have—

The man rubbed the amber fluid into her wound. Kristina felt it harden, filling the gash like quick-drying cement. The skin on her scalp grew taut and she gritted her teeth against the pain. The organic patchwork left her with a nauseating sense of invasive contact that rapidly spread to the rest of her body. Images flashed in her mind's eye, inchoate but striking: blasted landscapes that defied her understanding of spatial dimension; beings that looked like an extension of the tubular structure in the man's skull; a latticework of flesh and bone sheathing an entire planet.

The man smiled on his work, head tilted to one side. He picked up the hammer again, held it aloft—Kristina flinched—and as he brought it down, there was a loud pop, followed by a flash of white light. When the light faded, Kristina was alone on the floor, dazed, nauseous, heart racing, but alone. Several long moments passed in which her mind struggled to catch up with the events unfolding around her. Her breathing came in labored gasps. She stared, dazedly, at the ceiling. Finally, she rolled onto her hands and knees and vomited on the carpet. Once empty, she slowly got to her feet—using the rocking chair as leverage—only to collapse again, one knee splashing in the puddle of orange bile. She crawled the rest of the way to her bedroom, where her phone was charging. She needed to call someone. Needed an anchor to steady her unmooring reality. After some time—she suspected she lost consciousness more than once along the way—she reached the bedside table. As she groped for the phone, she saw the words NO SERVICE in the upper left-hand corner, and the last unread message was an emergency alert: IMPORTANT ADVISORY. STAY IN YOUR HOME. DO NOT GO OUTSIDE. She read the words twice before she lost consciousness again, and this time, she did not wake for several hours.

2

I have made a grave mistake. In my eagerness to create, I neglected to cover my tracks.

The Brutalists have followed me to this place and now my medium is damaged. They are a crude lot—a vastly different school of thought from my own. Of all the artists wandering the planet during this period of darkness, they are the most cruel and iconoclastic. They break and reshape, viewing physiological death as an essential part of their process. The unmaking is just as important as the remaking—it is a process, a performance, and, most of all, an abomination. I cannot bear to think what they have done to my medium. I must affect repairs before I can continue my great work. She is, after all, the only medium that will prove viable for my purposes—the only canvas capable of yielding a masterpiece.

She is prone on the bedroom floor. I roll her onto her back. Her blood oozes dark and thick around the vile filigree on her scalp. I must remove it. It will only interfere with my artistic vision. Extending a part of my essence, I smother the thing, severing its connection to the Brutalists. It softens, liquefies, and trickles down her forehead. Gently, I wipe it away. Behind me, in the living room, what little remains of the Brutalist—a shriveled, vaporous thing trembling under the couch—screams a final crescendo and slips back into the void.

I lift my medium from the floor—she floats up, weightless, arms and legs dangling, limp—and carry her to the bed. It does not take me long to rearrange the cellular structure within and around the wound. Soon, what was once broken is now whole—the fissure in her skull, the blood and budding lesion on her brain.

When I am finished, I let her sleep. She must recover before our next session. I will remain by her side until then, unseen, watchful, waiting.

I cannot let the Brutalists interfere again.

KRISTINA WOKE WITH THE DAWN. Her sleep had been deep but dreamless. The events of the previous evening were little more than a shivering, uncertain memory. And yet her anxiety remained. A dull persistent throb joined by the sensation that something was deeply and fundamentally wrong. She fought to control her breathing, recognizing the presages of a panic attack. As her wakefulness increased—and her awareness expanded—the pull of her anxiety became stronger. If only she could just go back to sleep.

Her hands went to her head, fingers massaging her scalp, inspecting for signs of damage. Nothing. A shiver passed through her body. *No. No. No. No. No*, her mind quailed. *This is wrong. I felt pain. I was bleeding.* She took a deep breath. Held it. Let it out in a vibrating rush. *Maybe it was all in my head. Another nightmare I twisted into some horrifying reality.* It had happened before—the holocaust of panic and delusion that lead to her diagnosis over ten years ago. Oddly, the memory calmed her somewhat. At least her illness was something she could understand. Understand and combat. She recalled, with sudden clarity, advice her therapist had given her, advice that had—over time—crystalized into a sort of mantra within her mind: *Think of your anxiety as a complex machine. If you don't commit to regular maintenance, it will fall into disrepair. Better to keep the gears oiled and the parts clean than take the whole thing apart when one component breaks down.*

It was an unnecessarily complicated metaphor for a simple concept. Anxiety lay at the heart of her condition. And as long as she found ways to curb and cope with it, she could avoid the manifestation of more serious symptoms. Of course, she had the assistance of antipsychotics and antidepressants, but—as her therapist often said—she needed to put in the effort as well. Her wellness was a work in progress from multiple fronts. If only she could remember that when things got particularly bad.

Her cellphone buzzed on the nightstand. Another emergency alert—or was that another component of her delusion? She leaned over, frowning. It was an incoming call from Gale. She seized the phone—caught a glimpse of her reflection on the black mirrored glass of the screen, dark stains around her eye sockets and over the bridge of her nose, stains like, no, don't think of that right now, you have no wound on your head, you're okay, there's nothing wrong—pressed the answer button, and held it against her ear. "Hello?" Her voice cracked. She cleared her throat. "Hello? Gale?"

"Kris, I can barely hear you." Gale sounded tinny and far away. "I just wanted to check in and make sure you're holding up all right."

Kristina bit her lip. Tears blurred her eyes. Even years after the divorce, Gale still made the effort to reach out, to ensure she was managing her illness, to inquire whether or not she was happy. Kristina was no longer her responsibility—her burden—and yet here she was, proving on some level that she still gave a shit. This act of compassion, or charity, or whatever it was, did not give Kristina hope of a rekindling what was lost—she had long since abandoned such reveries—but it did demonstrate to her that though their relationship had atrophied and died, there still remained a germ of empathy and friendship. The notion filled her with a combination of joy and unbridled sadness.

"I'm so happy to hear your voice," Kristina said. She sniffed loudly. "You don't know how much I needed to talk to someone right now."

"What's wrong? Did something happen?"

Kristina told her about the memory, the dream, or whatever the hell had happened with the false police officer. Spoken aloud, the event sounded like the rambling, nonsensical plot of a nightmare. Kristina felt her cheeks grow warm and her voice turn frantic with the telling. Gale listened as the weak cellular signal crackled and buzzed between them.

"And you think this was one of your episodes? Are you sure you weren't actually attacked?"

"I really don't know what happened."

"Do you need me to come over?"

She wanted desperately to say yes, but—

"No," she said. *It's not safe here.* "I'll be okay. I just need to hear your voice." She sniffed again, took a deep breath. Then: "Remember the anxiety machine?"

"Of course."

"While I have you on the phone, can you—" she trailed off, struck by a sudden pang of vulnerability. "—help me get things under control?"

"Yes. I think I can do that."

"Thank you."

She moved to the edge of the bed, stood up, waited for instruction. They had performed a similar routine many times before. Only now, they were separated by hundreds of miles of road and wilderness.

"Maybe start with the living room?"

Kristina obeyed. There was a puddle of dried vomit on the

carpet. The rocking chair was knocked askew. Her pillows on the couch bore the indentation of a seated body. The fibers would likely be pregnant with the policeman's strange odor—that stale, sulfurous stench. Kristina tightened her jaw, grinding her teeth painfully together. Something had obviously happened here, but what exactly? If the wound on her forehead had been the figment of a misfiring brain, what else was fabrication? And what was real?

"Kris, you there?"

"Yeah, sorry. I'm just freaking out a little."

"You're going to be okay," Gale said. "You just need to control your environment."

"I know," Kristina said too quickly. "Can I put you down for a second?"

"Of course."

She gripped the side of the couch and dragged it, grunting, toward the door. Bracing one end against the wall, she made certain it was impossible for anyone to gain entry. That should keep the false policeman—and the other interested parties he had mentioned—out of her home. This was her safe space, after all, her sanctuary—a modest realm within the bounds of her meager control. All she had to do was establish her dominance.

She picked up her phone again. "Okay, I'm back."

"What did you do?"

"Barricaded the front door."

Gale laughed good-naturedly. "You might want to lock the windows next."

Moving room to room, Kristina checked all the windows, making sure they were closed and locked, and as a final measure, lowered the blinds to block out the outside world. When she was satisfied with her fortifications, she placed pillows at the bottom of the picture window in the living room, opened the blinds a crack, and scanned the street.

"How is the machine running, now?"

"A little better. Thanks, Gale."

Outside, the neighborhood was necrotic with inactivity. No cars rolled down the street, no one walked their dog, and not even a solitary bird flitted among the trees. The view was quietly apoc-alyptic. *What is going on?* Kristina wondered. The words from the emergency alert flashed in her mind's eye: STAY IN YOUR HOME. DO NOT GO OUTSIDE.

"Are you going to be okay?" Gale asked after a prolonged, static-laden silence.

"I think so. I just want whatever this is to be over." She craned her neck and inspected the dust-covered husk of the ceiling light. "It's like everything that doesn't make sense proliferates in the dark. Like fungus. Or mold."

"Yeah, things have definitely been strange since the power went out."

"You think everything will go back to normal?"

"I fucking hope so."

They indulged in a moment of cathartic laughter. Then Gale said, "Call me if you need anything. You got this. You'll be okay. *We'll* be okay."

"We'll be okay," Kristina repeated with a smile on her lips, and the line went dead.

3

The longer I watch her, the more my empathy grows.

I have resolved to reach inside the secret places of her mind and extract the blemish that has plagued her for over ten years. I can erase her fear and anxiety; return to her existence a boon of easy, child-like joy. And around this reparation, her form will be remade into my greatest work thus far. I have never experienced such affection for a medium before. And I believe this love must be reflected in my approach and methodology.

I will continue my work tonight and reveal myself to Kristina. She cannot continue to believe she is living in a fabrication. She deserves the truth.

The time has come, at last, for the medium to meet its artist...

KRISTINA WOKE on her nest of pillows under the window to the sound of baying coming from the backyard. It did not sound like any animal she was familiar with, nor did it seem to originate from a human throat. The din was low-pitched—so low Kristina could feel it in her chest. If she had to compare it to anything, she might say it sounded like a sound artist had mingled and distorted the percussive barks of a large dog with the chirruping shriek of a tropical bird.

She cursed under her breath—*what the fuck now*—and got to her feet. Pins and needles rushed up and down her calves. The house was drenched in darkness, no moonlight piercing the slats in the blinds. She fumbled around for the headlamp, put it on and pressed the power button. The narrow beam revealed the living room in shades of blue and grey. She navigated the space, careful not to trip on pieces of furniture that had grown unfamiliar in the dark. At the rear sliding door, she cupped her hands against the glass and peered into the night. The tree line swayed almost rhythmically. The constant motion made it impossible to distinguish any potential source of the noise. Everything looked alive.

She unlocked the door, slid it open, and peered out. The wind sighed amongst the leaves, the stars and moon shone uncharacteristically bright in the sky. There were no artificial lights to dampen the display overhead. The view had always been breathtaking on her property. Since the blackout, however, the celestial vault glowed even brighter, constellations and the sweep of the Milky Way thrown into near blinding clarity. Kristina stepped out, head raised, eyes narrowed against the luminosity. She switched off her lamp to get a better view. It was then she noticed the red sphere of light moving across the stars.

"What is that?" she whispered aloud.

A branch snapped somewhere ahead. She swung her gaze to the tree line. An animal, limping, wounded, had pushed through the undergrowth, and was now moving in her direction. She almost turned and ran back into the house. But there was something familiar about this creature—the hanging jowls and sagging, expressive eyes. It looked somewhat like Barb, the basset hound her family had owned when she was a child. Barb had been dead and in the ground for over twenty-five years, but the thing that approached her now, could have been plucked from the same litter.

As it drew nearer, however, she realized that it wasn't wounded, not exactly. It looked incomplete, wrongly proportioned. One of its front legs divided at the knee joint into two separate limbs. It was missing the left hind leg, and the tail curled up and fused with flesh between its oddly pointed hipbones. One eye socket was riddled with small black eyes, while the other bore a single orb, tear-glossed and searching. *What the fuck was this thing? A deformed dog?* She gasped, took an involuntary step back.

Do not be afraid, said a voice inside her head.

She turned around to make sure someone hadn't entered the yard. She was alone. When she looked back at the tree line, the creature had drawn closer, and now sat lopsidedly a few paces away. It blinked up at her knowingly.

I will not hurt you, the voice said. It sounded oddly familiar.

"What are you?" Kristina said, hoarse with fear. "Are you like the policeman?"

No, the policeman seeks only to harm. I have come to help.

In spite of herself, Kristina found that she was laughing. Hands on knees, eyes pinched closed, lungs burning from the exertion. "I'm losing my fucking mind."

What you experienced is real. I am not your illness. Neither was the policeman. I repaired the wound on your head. I am here to help you.

Kristina nodded. Wiped a tear from her cheek. "A hallucination would say that."

Before she had time to react, the creature stood and pushed its head against her hand. Its coat was soft, warm, and on the instant of contact, she understood the voice was telling her the truth. She knew the reason behind the blackout, the intentions of the false policeman, the nature of the emergency alert. Everything resolved sharply in her mind, and her anxieties bled away until not even the slightest trace remained.

Exhausted from the truth and the unburdening of her anxiety, she slumped into the grass. The creature nuzzled her cheek, licked her with its oddly human tongue. *You are not broken. You are not lesser. Fate has been unfair to you. But I will make you better...*

SHE FOUND herself once again on the black marble slab from her dream. As before, the presence hung in the void overhead and the living statues watched the proceedings with unblinking interest. As she lay there, unable to move but relaxed, warm in spite of her nudity, she felt as though no time had passed between her dream and now—the intervening hours had shrunk into a meaningless clutter of events and impressions. The associated fear and panic were no more than vague memories.

She felt a warm touch against her cheek. A voice in her head asked if she was ready. She smiled and said she was. The hand then reached inside her and repaired, once and for all, the faulty machine rumbling and sparking at the center of her being. And for the first time in over ten years, Kristina Cameron knew no fear. On the edge of waking awareness, she sensed the lights coming on in the house in a brilliant shower of exorcising radiance.

EFFACE

LC VON HESSEN

In the wake of the working day, Jeannine prepared for the hunt. Neon flicker of the restaurant sign outside her Village window as she sat before the vanity. Bodycon black dress and thigh-high stiletto boots, a vinyl trenchcoat standing by to shield Jeannine from sidewalk catcalls. Jeannine, her hair teased out, lips, lids, and cheekbones painted to match the red, blue, violet baths of light in the ritual to come. The night cried out for Jeannine. The city reached out its clammy hands for Jeannine. My kingdom for a man after midnight. Or whomever, whatever, else struck her fancy.

Clok-clak-clok-clak-clok-clak of heels on pavement, one hand in her trenchcoat pocket, the other gripping the strap of her black clutch purse. Her club of choice, the Amour Fou, was within walking distance of her own apartment, a libertine's garden. As she turned the corner, a quintet of skinny girls emerged from the club, teetering in little tight dresses, bachelorette party sashes, and full-face plastic wolf masks. One by one, they raised their drunken heads and howled at the moon.

The broken light of the mirror ball casting its sequined shards above gyrating metallic peplum and neon geometry. Hissing fog cloaking walls and ceiling outfitted in the strict black-and-silver of fascists and fetishists. Hypnotic saxophone and synthesizer, faux-English accents and drum machines. Backlit silhouettes.

Hands of a stranger. Here Jeannine would dance in pointy boots until her toes contorted into Barbie-doll feet, until she could slip off the shoes and wrap her newly-bared calves around those of another. And who would it be tonight?

A slim and pretty New Wave boy awash in pastels, a curtain of hair flopping above one eyebrow, tossed back insouciantly? She'd seen him hungrily kissing a boy with a shaved head the week before, tugging at the O-ring of his dog collar. Now he turned his tender lips to hers, timid hands at her lower back. A warm bit of metal at his sternum, which she soon realized was a coke spoon.

Or would it be the bleach-blonde punk chick in a leather jacket and matching miniskirt, eyes smeared in coal or kohl? Her thigh in ripped fishnets between Jeannine's own, nudging against her lace panties. Her lipstick and Jeannine's meeting in a menstrual smear. Her tongue teasing the crucifix of Jeannine's black fashion rosary.

And across the room, a pair of eyes bored into her, eyes like drill bits. A pale face, lips lightly parted, unblinking. Shielded by the wide brim of a black hat. Perched atop a set of broad shoulders. An electric tremor shot through Jeannine, a frisson of arousal and fear.

But Jeannine was quickly knocked out of these thoughts. The punk chick winked and tugged her hand, leading her off the dance floor and trailing into a side room behind a clandestine door. For all the times Jeannine had ventured into this club, all the countless hours, she had never seen this door before.

Within this room, the neon of the dance floor gave way to the yellow glow of a single spotlight trained on a closed curtain. The space was long and narrow, a tight crowd of shadowed faces huddled around a runway backed by a stage. As she stepped forward, the footlights clicked on and the curtains swept back. Jeannine's hand was unclasped as her dance partner sought to squeeze closer to the runway, immediately disappearing in the dark.

All eyes were on the stage and the figure at its center, head cocked, arms bent, statue-stiff. *A doll girl*, thought Jeannine, for her face was concealed by the white ceramic mask of a pantomime tart, with heavy rouge and sea-green shadow and bright scarlet lips. She wore a baggy purple jumpsuit better suited to a clown, with a frilly Pagliacci collar and cuffs, hands concealed in white gloves and stockinged feet in black espadrilles. At no discernible cue, the doll girl began to move.

Slow and sleek, out of rhythm with the muffled beat seeping in through the door, she undulated down the runway. Though her motions bore no resemblance to the raucous bump and grind of burlesque, the fabric strips of her clown suit were gradually sloughed off with no touch of her fingertips, as if sheared away by invisible razors. Beneath, she wore a fringe-covered flapper dress, which soon pooled at her feet as well. The doll girl continued her dance in a satin teddy, torso and limbs concealed by a sort of porcelain couture, plate armor in the shape of a ball-jointed doll's body.

Despite this striptease, her movements were consistently more mesmeric than erotic, even as the lingerie dropped away to reveal a hairless body with vague nubs approximating nipples and a deep cleft like a lipless mouth in her bare, pallid crotch. Her head bent on its ball-joint neck, arms and legs twisted on their knee-and-ankle axes, as a normal human's could not. Was she actually a machine under there?

The doll girl's head turned to Jeannine, standing arms crossed in the corner, twin black pits of the mask's holes probing Jeannine's brown eyes. She paused only a moment as Jeannine, shivering, held her gaze; then she abruptly collapsed to the floor of the stage, strings cut. A smattering of tentative, nervous applause. The curtains dropped; the doll girl's body, hoisted backstage on unseen hands. The little theatre suddenly felt very humid with the great press of bodies.

Jeannine pushed through the door and saw the club unchanged: the disco ball spinning, the stereo pounding with jangling guitars, ample hairspray and makeup across genders.

And yet it now felt alien and detached, both a ruin of the past and an outlandish novelty for the tittering tourist. No longer a backyard garden, but a foreign land. She looked about for a familiar face. The punk girl was long gone, as were any friends, acquaintances, ex-lovers, regular bartenders. The crowd from the hidden theatre had not even followed her out. There was only one non-stranger left, and he was otherwise occupied.

"Oh, The Cockchafer? I don't go there anymore," shouted the New Wave boy into the ear of the waifish redhead whose arm encircled his waist. "I heard there was a serial killer." He lifted a hand to his throat and mimed strangling himself, to the redhead's stilted laugh.

She probably ought to go home.

Her path to the exit was temporarily blocked by a slumming crewcut preppie in a varsity jacket for which he was much too old.

"Got a light, dollface?"

His eyes slid down her boots and left a trail of slime. She bared her teeth at him and hissed like an asp.

Upon retrieving her trenchcoat from the coat check, Jeannine cinched its belt around her waist as she emerged into the night. The hand thrust into her left pocket immediately met a crumpled wad of paper. Smoothing it out under a streetlight, she found a flyer for a show, a flyer which she had never seen before: SENTINELLE, a production by MADAME FORTUNATA at AMOUR FOU above a crude Xeroxed image of a contorted wooden artist's dummy. MIDNIGHT SHARP.

It was now almost 1 in the morning.

She looked up from the flyer and caught the gaze of the masked man. The one who had stared so sharply, so intently, in the club. He was not simply pale and impassive in expression: his entire face was concealed by a white mask, plain of any adornment. He wore a black fedora and a black trenchcoat down to the ankles, buttoned up to the neck, hands tucked into his pockets. He stood at the entrance to an alley several yards down the block, as if waiting for someone.

Waiting for her. To see him.

And when she had seen him, their locked eyes undeniable proof, he nodded and backed into the alley like a trail of cigarette smoke.

A fresh burst of cold sweat at the thought of what he must be. A plainclothes policeman. A Soviet spy.

But what had she *done?*

In this city she was no one, anonymous. In the daylight she worked at an office to finance her basic needs and her nights. And at night she only wanted to have fun.

MADAME FORTUNATA HAD BEEN BORN with the current century and resided for much of that time on the Upper West Side. Yet her decor, Jeannine learned upon being buzzed in, was surprisingly ultramodern. A shag carpet of lavender-lilac. A pair of dividing walls made of frosted glass cubes. Twin rows of track lighting shining down on the wall-mounted art like interrogators' spotlights. Floating grids and scalene triangles, wavy lines and zigzags in muted peach and turquoise, in coral and aquamarine, in fuchsia and electric blue. The cobra eyes, pallid skin, and white ghastly grin of a Patrick Nagel print looming across the back wall. That simplified, softened, pastel-and-neon iteration of Deco.

Jeannine flashed back to the omnipresent dun dead brown of the suburbs she had escaped. Plastic and Bakelite and vinyl siding in faux wood grain. A simulacrum of rustic organic matter. A failed attempt to get back to the land from which the identical houses had sprung. Jeannine preferred artifice that acknowledged what it was.

Madame Fortunata's decades of accomplishments hung on the walls to either side of the long entry hall. Framed posters boasted of collaborations with Diaghilev's Ballets Russes, Pina Bausch's Tanztheater, the Graham Company here in Manhattan, the Markos Company in Berlin, and several itinerant Japanese troupes featuring something called *bunraku.* In recent years she had withdrawn from the public, citing a decline in health, and unofficially retired.

Jeannine was not a connoisseur of choreography and would not have recognized the name: had in fact previously known

Madame Fortunata only by her government name. This was how the choreographer had found her, sought her out, though they had never directly spoken or interacted face-to-face: an embossed invitation on her desk, paired with an uptown address, and here she was.

For the grand Madame was, it turned out, a client of Jeannine's firm in that daylight world of starched collars and shoulder pads, tanned and toned princes of commerce. Knights in shining Armani. Yet in truth they were only smarmy yuppies snapping their suspenders like old-time carnival barkers and robber barons chomping on a fat *cee*-gar, certain anyone could be had for the right price, the right mix of flash and glitz. This did not matter to Jeannine. These men were so much detritus to her. The subway rats were better company.

At odds with the decor was a small framed sepia photograph dated 1905, which she stepped closer to inspect. Her hostess, she assumed, as a young girl, head topped by thick bangs and lop-sided bow, chin tilted low like a Kubrick villain with a shy, awkward smile, clutching a naked bisque baby doll to her pinafore. A tall man's large hand rested on her small shoulder, his dark trouser leg and wingtip a Doric column to her right, the rest of him cropped out of frame. A work bench stood behind her, covered in wood shavings, paintbrushes, hand tools, and doll parts.

"Come in, dear," the Madame beckoned. "Come in, Miss Jeannine."

A creaky scythe-rasp in her voice. A hint of accent Jeannine couldn't place shrouded in well-worn Manhattanese. She followed the source of the voice and stepped through the glass dividing walls.

And was instantly taken aback. The walls at either side of her were entirely covered with masks and little clowns and harlequin dolls, hanging from nails or set into niche tableaux. Stranger still, many dolls sprang to life as she stepped forward, as though she had tripped a hidden sensor. The muffled sound of whirring clockwork behind the violet walls. Tilting their heads, slowly, carefully, almost tentatively moving their shrunken arms and legs. A few moved on fixed platforms, cut-paper *commedia* stages in which a gleaming devil surprised a girl in her boudoir, a ballerina rotated on a single toe, a grimacing man in a tricorne and breeches chased a buxom woman clutching a tumor-shaped baby.

But above all, the masks. Phallic-nosed, swollen-cheeked Carnevale masks. Comedy/Tragedy masks conjoined at the cheek like Siamese twins. Jesters with a vertical slash down each eye, remnants of the King's displeasure. Ingenues with widened eyeholes above startled or fellatious O-mouths. Masks wearing masks, metallic Mardi Gras dominoes. Colorful ribbons dangling to either side, never to knot around a human face. Delicate half-veils of fashionable midcentury widows. Sigil-like scribbles, black tears and stars, diamonds and music notes dotting cheeks and chins like the velvet *mouches* donned by courtiers to conceal smallpox and syphilis scars. The heavy shadow, lipstick, and rouge of players for the stage and ladies of the night. Open sockets and flat mouths: plaintive, coquettish, conspiratorial, sneering.

Sequins and gold braid. Satin and lamé. Tulle and lace. Feathers and rhinestones. Porcelain, plaster, white-glazed ceramic. Women, children, androgynes. Jokers and mimes, flappers and courtesans, frozen in time.

The famous choreographer sat on the carpet between these walls in a violet-black leotard cut high over knobby hip bones, knees bent like a mantis. Thin calves disappearing into woolly leg warmers, stamens rich with pollen. Head crowned with ample silver-grey hair, pinned back in a lavender rinse.

"Aubergine," she said, spreading an arm to indicate her wardrobe, her decor, all of it. "The color of royalty. The hue of the gods."

Her voice was slightly muffled, emitting as it did from behind, yes, a white mask. A mask to shield a lifelong performer's vanity over her aging features? But no, it was more than that facile, potentially sexist explanation. The mask, with its pastel pools of faux makeup, its thin, knowing arched eyebrows, wore a placid expression enigmatic enough to read as curious or domineering.

"Some tea?" She fanned her long fingers toward a teapot and a pair of cups on a low stool at her side. Jeannine gave her assent and sat down cross-legged on the thick carpet, attempting to ignore the scrutiny of all those pale faces.

"You enjoyed my girl's performance at the Amour Fou."

An uneasy nod from Jeannine.

Madame Fortunata lifted a teacup and held it up to her mask's closed mouth, tipping it politely before setting it back on the stool. The cup was empty. A pantomime. A farce.

A tea party, thought Jeannine. *A child's tea party.* Tiny seats around a playroom table stuffed with piebald bears and slouching Victorian dollies with stovepipe curls and terrible hints of bared, tiny teeth. She thought of the little girl in the sepia photo: perhaps behind the mask hung a kindergartener's face on the body of an octogenarian.

"I thought you might take interest in a private performance of a new production I have been working on. My own little ensemble. Fellow creatures of the night, like yourself. Girls, women, boys."

"And men," Jeannine added reflexively, to intrusive thoughts of the tall man in the white mask.

A sudden chill from her hostess led to several moments of loaded silence. An air of disapproval in the gleaming features of Fortunata's mask.

"No, no men. *Never* men."

Fortunata cocked her head like the stringless marionette girl of Sentinelle.

"You look familiar somehow. Outside of the office, of course." (But she had never seen Jeannine before, not at the office at least. She always sent an underling to relay documents back and forth, a small, short person, possibly a grandchild, who wore a hooded raincoat no matter the weather and said nothing.) "Have you recorded a tape for a video dating service?"

"No?" That was truly a *no*, period, but she was taken aback at such a random query.

"You are young," her hostess said, leaning forward, "And I'll offer you some advice.

"A woman I knew met a man, a famous actor, through a personal ad. An eccentric man. I needn't say his name; I suspect you would know him. Handsome, you know, but very stern. He showed up with a tan trenchcoat all buttoned up and a matching fedora. He looked like a newspaperman.

"She had a loft in Tribeca, and he came to her there and they… why, you're a modern girl, I won't mince words. They made love. He took her to bed, and he made love to her. And he was a diligent lover. Good with his tongue. But he kept his suit on the whole time, and only unbuttoned his trousers.

"He left afterward: he'd told her he had an early call time the next morning. Actors, you know. And she was still in her negligee basking in it all when she realized he had left his umbrella behind. So she went after him, down into the subway. And she found his face on the subway tracks.

"Yes, his *face*. She saw that grubby thing on the tracks and hooked it up with the umbrella, and held it in her hands. It was a lifelike rubber mask. He was still on the platform, standing against a support pillar and lighting a cigarette, and she saw him. His real face was all burnt away, with no nose, like a skeleton. The flesh was raw, like he had peeled off his own skin. And his teeth, his bare teeth, all yellow in the red gums.

"Of course it wasn't the actor at all. It really *was* a newspaperman. He merely wanted to collect gossip material for the newspapers. And for blackmail.

"The moral is: Never trust a *face!*"

And with that she thrust another invitation into Jeannine's hands.

She examined the envelope as she boarded the elevator. The same Xeroxed artist dummy from the Sentinelle flyer had been duplicated several times. This show bore the ridiculous name: Slice Me Nicely.

Through the lobby windows, night had fallen, yet it was only afternoon when she had arrived. She had only stayed long enough for half a teacup. Time had folded without her consent.

On the sidewalk before the building was the masked man.

Waiting for her. Following her. He nodded and saluted, spreading his arm in invitation.

Jeannine, locked in an instant trance. Jeannine, gliding forward to take his hand. That hand completely hidden within a ceramic glove, just as the mask concealed his entire head and neck. Jeannine and the masked man, waltzing among the fallen leaves.

All automotive and foot traffic faded away. No longer pavement under their heels but polished marble and brass. A music box couple in a glistening chapel of gilt and mirror. Revolving across an automaton mainspring to the haunting tune of a barrel organ. How simple it is, to relinquish control.

His embrace tightened as the dance progressed. Across her forehead and cheek came a stirring breeze, the gentle breath from his mouth slit and the discreet holes for his nostrils. And far lower still, an uncommon firmness pressed against her through their respective trenchcoats. Why, he need only unbutton them both and lift her up in his strong arms in order to—

At this flush of arousal she blinked, once, to find herself standing alone in the cold wind. Pedestrians turned their eyes to her curiously, then walked on, indifferent.

JEANNINE WORE sensible heels to Slice Me Nicely. If asked, she would be unable to articulate why she was going at all. The invitation tugged her along like a fish with a hook through its gills.

Following Fortunata's invitation at the appointed date and time led Jeannine to a warehouse in Chelsea, a warehouse like any other. She was, strangely, alone on this block. Her destination made itself known by a chorus of rhythmic mechanical creaks that increased in volume as she stepped through the open door.

She was bathed in yellow-gold lighting from lamps affixed to skeletal girders. The site of the performance made little attempt to camouflage its industrial origins, a warehouse turned construction site long abandoned to roaches and rust. Across the bare floor and sparse furniture were scattered various drapes, tapestries, and sheets of rumpled plastic and colored cellophane, as if replicating the aftermath of a raucous party; but for the most part the space lay bare, from its stripped foundations and overhead fluorescents to the illusory nudity of half its performers. This was an interactive piece, an experimental performance: no stage, one only walked amongst the dancers and their choreographed motions. Through inclination or instruction, they fully ignored her.

Jeannine could best describe this as an impotent orgy. Performers in unitards with crudely smeared greasepaint across their faces and bodies feigned theatrical intercourse with statues and automatons and sometimes each other: bumping blunted, sexless mannequin bulges together, or rutting in feigned ecstasy against a dressmaker's dummy. They need not even have humanoid partners: one dancer, on elbows and tiptoes, jerked her pelvis against a metal support beam.

In the room's rough center was Madame Fortunata: or, at least, a reasonable simulacrum. Her head was encased in a seamless plastic plum. She wore the same outfit of her prior meeting with Jeannine but perhaps it wasn't her, perhaps it was a younger body, a bit more flesh on the bones, nothing spotted or sagging on her hands and neck, which were the only visible sources of skin. She performed a set series of conductorial motions from the waist up, all uncomfortably unnatural: too slow, too jerky, too *wrong*.

In fact quite a bit looked *wrong* to Jeannine. There was no joy in this show. Many performers crudely dance-fucking were sickly figures with exhausted, weathered faces, their costumes encrusted with suspicious white, red-brown, and yellow stains. Some, indeed, had the slackened black lips and shriveled eyelids of cadavers. One humped the jutting ribcage of a skinned animal impaled on a metal spike programmed to jostle chaotically away. Another's large abscess had popped under her unitard from her exertions with a CPR dummy and a steady stream of pus dripped in a puddle on the cement floor as she humped.

Jeannine stepped backward to avoid the spreading pool and

accidentally jostled a human dancer: yes, she was certain she felt the cushioning smack of thinly-clothed flesh. Turning around, mumbling an apology, she saw that the dancer's thigh had cracked open, revealing thick red cuts of cold meat packed around a metal piston within a casing of glazed clay. The dancer continued to gyrate, grinning at Jeannine too broadly below unblinking eyes.

There was no audience. There were no other guests. It was only a show for Jeannine. For Jeannine alone.

She fled the warehouse and sought a taxi. Back home, immediately. Back to safety and certainty.

In her apartment that night, she ran a warm bath to soak off the night's madness. The closest she could come to a swim unless she wanted to dive into the water at Coney Island and emerge a pincushion of discarded junkie needles.

JEANNINE SUPPOSED the water had lulled her to sleep, for she awoke in a tub that had grown four claw feet and a layer of gilt, strewn with pink and red rose petals from a bouquet she hadn't bought.

The man in the white mask was in her apartment. The tall, broad-shouldered man in the white mask, standing in the next room. The bathroom door was shut but she knew, could sense his presence. He had come to her room at night through the nonexistent French doors to the nonexistent balcony. (What was it, really? She dimly recalled a stubborn window onto a rickety fire escape.) She did not fear his entrance: it was, somehow, expected.

Donning the black lace-trimmed silk slip and matching robe she knew she would find hanging from the door, she stepped into the room before him, flatteringly dark but for the light of the city seeping in through the windows. Her modest fold-out bed had sprouted four posters and a sheer canopy. He stood with hands clasped, legs spread apart, in the gap of the open French doors, like a palace guard. He nodded low, tipped his hat, and spread his arms to greet her. To invite her.

The man slipped off his trenchcoat, beneath which he wore nothing but knee-high black riding boots. His hands were the same porcelain gloves, the molded hands gently cupped for caressing, index fingers cocked just so. With these hands he slid the straps down over her shoulders, cool trails on her skin. She felt his breath, unmistakably cold, but could not hear him breathing. Her lips and cheek against his mask, the mask which he did not remove, nor did she so attempt. No seam, no latch, no knot, no zipper. She could picture nothing beyond his strikingly molded, even features.

She lay across black satin sheets, pressed into the mattress by his strong body, impossibly cold and smooth, false skin painted glossy white, tinted blue, violet, red under the neon bleed from the sign outside. Her nails could not rake or dig in. Even his erection was lacking the pliance of flesh. At his first slow thrust she had to wait for and will her body to settle its membranes around him lest she cleave in two, *slice me nicely*. He thrusted with unblinking eyes. He came silently. A rush of copious seed, thick and opaque, like paste.

And she climaxed in a blaze of white.

Jeannine awoke alone on her fold-out bed, still folded in to resemble a couch with assorted throw pillows. Her mind's eye could only view the fragmented memory of the man's visit through the vaseline-smear of a soap opera, so dreamlike it could scarcely have happened. But her body remembered: the little aftershocks, the pleasant ache. The spilt batter staining the fabric.

So dreamlike she hadn't thought to ask for a condom. She hadn't thought to speak at all.

At the office, a loaded staleness in the air, much heavier than usual. A brown and beige suburban creep within the city walls.

She stared at the constant wink of the green cursor on the computer monitor. Pixel tally marks like centipede legs. Accounts

Payable Ronnie, self-appointed office jester, knocked on the cubicle wall, cracking the same tired joke: *You know what the calendar says? Big Brother is Watching*. He'd been doing it since New Year's and it wasn't funny then either. The screeching motions of the copy machine, the dot-matrix printer, an awful ballet of electronics.

At the Amour Fou, none of the bartenders, staff, or regulars knew a thing about the performance of Sentinelle, the doll girl in the mask, or the presence of a secret theatre. Nor could she find the theatre door, even with the house lights up: no discreet frame flush with the wall like a servants' entrance. She'd expected nothing else. The city's magic had been siphoned from the night.

But worst of all was the disturbingly rapid swell of Jeannine's abdomen, far, far faster than the result of a normal accident. It could not be strapped down with normal shapewear or dismissed as a temporary souvenir of junk food and hormones. Certainly not when the growing curve felt as stiff as set plaster under the outer cushion of skin. When she could knock on her stomach and hear a hollow echo. A sloshing inside. Like a half-empty jar of preserves.

No, *no*. The clinic must look after all this. Absolutely not. No babies, no motherhood for Jeannine, and certainly not alone. She had been with more than one man in the previous month, yet she knew, *she knew* who was the cause of this trouble.

Thus an appointment was quietly booked over the phone for one chilly afternoon.

And thus, while heading briskly down the sidewalk to that appointment, a gloved hand darted from the alley and pressed a chemical-drenched rag over her mouth.

"—HIS FACE?"

Deep-set eyes glowered above in a ghost-pale face with closed lips.

"Did you see his face?" she hissed at Jeannine, the bound and paralyzed patient, caught in the sickly beam of a yellow spotlight.

But Jeannine could not answer: this the older woman knew.

Madame Fortunata raised her hand, fingers fanning upward, and Jeannine's stomach split open bloodlessly, as if on piano wire. The masks and harlequins looked on in the dark, whispering amongst themselves, little students in a surgical theatre.

She could only stare as the choreographer plunged her long fingers into Jeannine's abdomen. Jeannine's body, full of thick white fluid coating her innards, already congealing in the open air.

After much careful rooting around, Fortunata emerged, dripping, with the litter. Blank-faced and sexless white doll-bodies slowly squirming in her bony hands. Bobbing, silent mouths, as they had neither stomachs nor vocal cords. Soon enough they would don jesters' caps and diamond jumpsuits and join their cousins on the walls.

But Fortunata was not finished.

She reached down, behind Jeannine's ears, and removed her face.

She held it up for the patient to view, of course: she was not a *monster*. The face, Jeannine's face, took the form of a blue plastic Tragedy mask. As the stale air nestled on Jeannine's exposed muscles and teeth, she thought she saw the empty patch of wall where the face would reside.

Then Madame Fortunata slipped her spider-fingers to the back of her skull to untie her own face—and most cruelly of all, Jeannine was allowed to remember.

ART MURMUR

GARY J. SHIPLEY

I HAVE ONE OF THOSE FACES PEOPLE SEE EVERYWHERE. HALF GOD, HALF devil: my halo grows fangs. I'm missing a missing tooth. With all three primary stressors, I'm overloaded with reasons why they're dead. And poor Michael too, now, by his own hand. Suicided through guilt, like that was a thing. (If you can't live with yourself, live with someone else instead: my example is here to be followed.) Did everyone just up and forget how to forget? And so what if my sister arranged for a car to take me across the border. Did nobody ever have a sister? Do people not every day digest the indigestible?

I have one of those faces people see everywhere, a face you can't see through or around. An onion-skinned face, garlic-smeared to preserve the like for like. I hide my scars with a pearl choker; you see about as much of me as you do Édith Scob, face-fail after face-fail. The price of rejecting the faces of the dead is having no face at all. I became just one more species of chameleon in Madagascar. All the lemurs I could eat. I got schooled in isolation: 88 million years of it. (Never want for quiet that quiet.) I tried to recruit for L'eglise de Philedelphia, for Christine and mama; but no one was having it, no one into a religious cult they couldn't fuck their way out of.

In near constant sunshine, gods hide in damp spaces, in dicks, like fleas. They say Emmanuel loved me: an unconsummated, unrequited love. They give me no facility to love my best friend. We go grey. We are lovebirds where they can't see us. Our grey heads in a vice thinking the same one thought. Beautiful godless coma of causes. I have unrequited consciousness of who you are. You don't scare me: I'm inanimate with pain. If your family isn't soil, you cannot know. If you haven't actually done what you always thought would remain that way, the thing so huge you get lost inside it, then you cannot understand. It's beyond you, beyond space-time; I'm rewriting the entire cosmology of why the future kills. SpaceX took my brain to the moon, brought it back in the shape of a footprint.

When I dream of volcanoes, it's not Vesuvius I see but Mons Rümker, like when I buy my favorite monkey meat in Belgium, and spit it out for the magpies to nosh. You know this tendency toward defacement (or do I mean displacement?) is killing me, right? Creepy how that spate of wincing at the who and what of myself should result in this exact cross-infection of personages. All this needless babble in folded space. Skinned rabbits dragging their fur back on, eyes and mouths kept open with toothpicks. All of our centuries loop on this moment, this moment of fatty dreams and frightened seagulls splayed, swooning. The filthy broth of the sky. The unknown children. The unknown wives.

I depend on the disease of any part of any body. Some fool's disease. We come together in terms of convenience. Our too-perfect sanity a promiscuity of opposites, so promise me convulsions and religious excitement, because years later nothing will have changed. Strangers will still be asking for directions to the nearest parodic consecration, to the gallery of galleries, the quintessence of stupidity around what corner, because Baudelaire, because art must be stupid, because I am the exemplary moron, and because my subjects are one now and dead, my afflatus airless, my muses merged and murky without a sound.

My art is so many words. My art is this wall, this thickening of space. A brain with too much plasticity will render you helpless; I'm a nascent jelly in search of a mould, a cortical bulge drooling from a pressure crack in my skull a few millimeters inside the right scoop of my receding hairline. You can't bring the dead back to life with a sonorous inflection. Walls and screens are not bodies. Like this we are all blessed, the world merciful after all. I now know murder is a clumsy instrument for redescribing my frustrations with ultimate secular meaning, but we work with what we have.

I come to think of them as merely apostrophic, and them the same about me. I think of them the way a prisoner would his next conjugal visit: a place in the wider world in which to place myself, to establish some corporeal connection, albeit contrived, albeit destructive, cruel, and painful. Life outside the abstract's such a strenuous dupery.

I'm pursued. I hide away. I wanted the future, so I killed my family. It seems I've murdered so many young things, scarcely born some of them – and yet already too old before I started. There is only the problem now of what comes next. I make a kind of *Bilderatlas* (you remember Aby Warburg?) for something that never existed. My family is a lie; my dead family is a lie. I use my head as a coal hammer, smash it over and over. I read de Selby's *The Layman's Atlas* out of the thinnest, skinless air. I'm here for the solution to the impossibility of the new: an atlas of nowhere and of nothing.

I add to the walls every day; it's my way of moving beyond them, of turning my defoliated family tree into something living. Embracing my indecency, I take heed of Crevel, and no longer spend my life getting old. I am iterative the way liquids are iterative, the way blood seeped from their vacated heads before I covered them up, before the sight of them turned supplemental to certain baseline empathies, before their performative hiatus excreted an unsanitary mesh of proto-realities beyond the control of even my flair for virtuosic elision. How can I make art out of them? How can I not?

These walls are my plumage, my floofy epigenetic coif, my lustral monomania. Reality does not come close. I insulate: my acquisitive tendencies escalating to the point of depleted muscle mass and sensory suffocation. Only with my invagination complete will I breathe again, see again, move again, the remains of my crushed organs spontaneously rejuvenated in the finely tuned centricity of this one true work of art.

I make a wall like every obsessive makes a wall, by adorning an already existing wall with all the fragments of my obsession: photographs, pages of highlighted and encircled text, connecting strings, newspaper clippings, maps, timelines, rainbow cork board pins scattered in discursive yet meaningful arrangements. It will be my wall of failure: of the men I didn't apprehend, the prostitutes I never killed, the convicts I never rescued, the banks I never robbed. My wall of disquiet. I will keep adding to it until I am forced to include adjacent walls. It will spread like a fungal infection. I'll place a viewing seat at some precisely measured distance, where I'll sit for hours studying what I've done (by failing to do anything). There will also be tables with computer monitors, at least three, probably four, similarly-sized, playing looped videos of things and people pertinent to the investigation – the investigatory detritus of my non-investigation – to which my eyes will travel when the stillness of the wall becomes oppressive.

On the wall, down by the skirting, is a photograph of Paul McCarthy shitting into his own mouth. There's the big white beard, the cap; I'm sure it's him. I wrote his name on the back. It's there to remind me of something, but I'm not sure what. It will come to me. Sometimes one of the monitors will play snippets of *Painter* or *Experimental Dancer*. I sourced them from UbuWeb and they help to contextualize the seriousness of the wall. Above that same monitor are photos of my family: five separate portraits, five separate smiles – one of them a little off (as if maybe they knew). Pinned next to them is Lorca's "New York (Office and Denunciation)," where I have underlined the many of those that smash the sky to bits. Some might consider this juxtaposition bad taste, but it's all in keeping with the provocation of the wall itself.

The crazy wall is an extension of the investigation or crime board – often referred to as simply *the board* – and the crazy room an extension of that. I guess, the thing is, I want too much of everything to the point that I settle for less than I started with. I sit in my chair and smoke and look at what I've amassed. I just sit and smoke and think, as if an answer is on the way. As if the answer that arrives won't be a further irritation, another irresolute itch in some inaccessible area of the bodies we're trying so hard to sleep inside. We are mangy in our chairs. I think of it as a kind of theology of moments, a laboratory of furtive howling. I hear myself talking in some unknown dialect. I voice as if from a lurching sea.

The meaning of futility is such a delicate thing. The appetite that consumes itself. The vampiric consumption of my thick French blood. The one question that never goes away: What am I avoiding? Everything a distraction from whatever the answer is, but then the answer's not there. Or it's straightaway lost among the trees, with the forest on fire, with the squirrels turned to charcoal, with my yellowing eyes and skin, my failing liver.

I could be heard developing a belly. Sleeping vertically, suspended by my feet. The irrelevance of a disposition.

I have to get out of here: I'm forgetting the weather. What do I have to do to become intolerable to myself? There was a moment right before I shot one of them, I forget which, when the rifle bullet itself seemed so very precious. Such a weird concentration of emotion in such an inert lump of metal. People will say it's displacement, but they weren't there. No one was. Even I wasn't there, not really.

I sometimes like to imagine I'm holed up in an apartment in some dilapidated project in America. I look at pictures of them and see myself on the other side of one of the windows. I never go out. I have a silly amount of locks and chains on the front door; it would be easier to come in through the walls. I keep pictures of the best ones pinned up in a row: Queensbridge Houses, Robert Taylor Homes, Magnolia Projects, Pruitt-Igoe, Cabrini Gree, Hotel Iveria, Avalon Gardens, and Imperial Courts. If I live there it's because it's too dangerous to go out. I immerse myself in something insanely abstract and esoteric. I live inside whatever it is I'm doing, and barely eat or sleep because of it. Sometimes it's an art form so intricate and extravagant that nobody has ever come close. Other times it's a philosophical theory so convoluted and arcane that it fills thousands of pages of tiny spidery script and hand drawn diagrams that would take a lifetime for anyone else to decipher. I imagine the same thing contained in just a few lines, the brilliant simplicity of which will belie the decades I spent searching for it. Surpassing the Duchampian revolution in art, this discovery will reconfigure the very fabric of human meaning. It will make it mean something. No one will ever again wonder why it is their senescence feels so vicious.

At a certain time on a certain day, at a train station in Paris, I could see in people's faces how they didn't want to do this anymore. They'd soaked up their lives and were full with every new kind of emptiness. I followed the rules. I refrained from smoking. I didn't talk to anyone. I took my secrets to the grave – the one in Fourqueux, unmarked, posing like nature. I swallowed all the acorns. What was left but waiting? The meditation exercise at the top of my voice. And then nothing. No saplings in sight. Only bad guts and a mutilated tree, and the young trees that refused to grow, because my stomach wasn't soil, wasn't a labyrinth of nutrients, but thin air, the sedimented nothing of my habits.

I glom what life I can from this infinite fatigue. What kind of man prays in every direction at once? I'm clammy to the bone. Let us alone with our technology and our sorrow. Our sorrow without history. Our history prescinded from our insulated state.

I've spent these years in a shrinking room running my brain through a meat slicer only so I can piece it back together again. And only now do I feel ready to turn failing upwards into an art.

It's like I'm John Holden in *Night of the Demon* when I need to be Julian Karswell. But I'm also the John Holden that nothing happens to. No demon arrives at night at the behest of an enigmatic devil-worshipper – unless the walls themselves are demons, and they are, of course they are. Everything is theory till the end. I attend my conference and nobody gets scared, because nobody really believes. I'm scared all the time now, because all I have is what must happen but won't because it can't, but will and must and at any time or never but soon...

I regret that art must say something even when it deliberately says nothing. I regret that art does not have anywhere near enough regrets. My art is I regret art. The art of this regret is that the only thing it leaves behind, as its remainder, is itself art. But the future of art is not more art. The future of writing is not more writing. The future is more and more becoming less and less. The future is luxury masquerading as need. It's a baby born inside years of swallowed vomit. It has more than two heads; it has heads like we have hair. I say *we* as if I hadn't shaved mine off, as if my scalp isn't a disguise, as if the walls now weren't too close to externalize my flailing arms, my running legs. The bodies of ma famille resurrected in this airless chamber of what's left, the artwork consuming all physical space, everything outside growing farther away. Adieu because I feel them now. Adieu because it's time.

No more room. No more air. No more. All of it.

I hear toneless, monotonous voices. They say I'm difficult to keep alive, like orchids. They sound like the legs on a mechanical frog. The speakers are sick and their voices sometimes wordless, with long pauses between one sound and the next. I specialize in not falling asleep. Behind my eyes there's just this blue vapor, the maladroitly forged ontology of another world citing names as substances to touch. With my eyes shut I am all the drains of history. The waste of all of it flowing through me, cumulating in some imagined blockage to form the ultimate daydream. My thoughts agglutinative and stood on end, vertical without stopping.

ALL THE RAPES IN THE MUSEUM

JOE KOCH

THEN BY DIVINE INSIGHT I KNEW YOU WERE MORE THAN ANOTHER VICTIM
dumped in my cell. Disguised as one more mute shaking in the
corner—for many have passed in the years or minutes I have
survived this lightless dungeon—at first you refused me.
Choosing to shudder nude in the damp hay as if the garb of
human warmth I offered was tincture of strange poison, bearing
witness to my tests when put to the question and suffering likewise in yours; you through the drama of our trials revealed a slow
mystery. Mirrors of tortures borne, we cracked the cold silence of
the plane dividing us when you left your suit of corporeal illusion
to enter the iron maiden and commune with me.

Heretic, remember when my fingers walked upon your skin
like Lilliputian legs, traversing your torso, nape, and spine,
exploring every inch of your trembling in the long cold dark
between interrogations? You were my promised land. I dwelled in
you with my forbidden tongue's intent, with a language of
creation burning away the euphemisms that normalize violence,
with your figure fingered into hierarchical revenge.

My knifeless Spartan queen between assaults, you gave me
respite in the steady pain of your brutal consistency, in the many
needles of your open arms. One door to the left; one door to the
right; both closed to clasp me in a deadly embrace as if we could
cocoon as one. The tips of your needles pressed feathers into my

skin from forehead to belly to feet, and body captive on those trembling, sharp, and relentlessly present pinpoints I began to see—to really, truly see—the wings withheld in yours.

Your gift of surprise, magic of compassion; yes, it's true. I was ready to give up. Ready to die. We were broken, chipped, and faded. Our martyred cracks could never be restored. Together beset by many rapes, we both knew the futility of this endless investigation. We knew none escaped these chains once they were swallowed up and sunk deep inside the hidden bowels of this museum where accusation equals guilt.

The institution stripped us. They made us watch. Where there were shadows, they shined a bright light to expose our aesthetic flaws. When in agonized resistance at knife point I turned away from the sight of the seventh soldier drilling his syphilis into your limp collapsing form, his armor clattering as his gut heaved back and forth, his unwashed buttocks clenching and unclenching, his hateful thrusts breaking what was already broken in you; when I at last turned away in defiance and they pressed the edge of the blade to my throat and my carotid artery thumped against the metal and the metal warmed; when they said watch or we'll kill you, we'll kill you and fuck your dead body, I said *Good*, for I had learned that much of their language.

I looked them in the eyes and I said *Do it*.

No buoyant slash released me. These same foreign pale men who claimed the bravery of god-like judgement and reveled together homogenized in god-like exercise of power proved too small of will to shoulder the due burden of my murder. The silent violence of their secrecy exceeded the blunt violence of their abuse. They would delegate my death.

They locked me inside the iron maiden. This device shaped like a welcoming cocoon embraced me with her ineluctable threat. The right door closed first, and then the left. Both doors closed over my screaming face.

I trembled on the points of many spikes and dared not move lest my vulnerable body suffer countless impalements. The cocoon was tightened at intervals, moving the spikes closer to the surface of my skin each day or hour or minute. I no longer understood time. Weakness from starvation and my terror of slumping in my sleep poised my enfeebled flesh tensely across the tips of the iron needles. The metal pressed. Slow punctures emptied my veins, my bladder, my hissing lungs; the damp cold of the dungeon became raging heat as fever flared in my wounds and my obstinate physical instincts preserved me, rejecting infection from the many stinking holes. You also stank, my dead angel, my fallen one, a slumped corpse left for horrific edification that I might witness an example of my own imminent decay.

More time passed. The cocoon tightened again, again. And behold!

You came.

From your muteness into speech of the body, speech of elixir from flesh and radiant hallucinogenic poisons no longer strange but gilded, illicit, and certainly sacred, you comforted me. Angel or demon undefined, you came *from*, *through*, and *with* death. You left your shadowed corpse and met me without fear. Perhaps you are not an angel of god but an angel of death. I don't know.

I don't care.

And truly, brashly, unapologetically—though it may be impossible and unwise—I welcome you with memory clear and fond awareness of my full acceptance anew every time you come to surprise me and share with me yet another death.

I match my form to yours in carnal gestures, my imprisoned fingertips now free to trace the planes of a lucid geometry once concealed in life from the hunger of my touch; but no more, no more. These golden means of rigid anatomy fondle free in death. Here are your wings. This is your crown of many feathers. These are your many unblinking eyes. Wisdom may from misfortune and with unexpected grace assume a forbidden and monstrous disguise.

Confined and combined—in the cocoon of the iron maiden for months or days or minutes, we feasted on the raw energy of our newborn masticating flesh. We grinded our starved palates against a liminal and vast want; sipped the cup of our sex-gushed sweat, saliva, and tears. We grew obscenely drunk on the excess of our liquid macerations. We thrived without need of any natural sustenance outside the scorched fumes of our nutritious dying bodies.

I saw the truth of you in your sudden and unexpected comprehension of lust, a lust essential in our rebellion against torture. When we died, what remained of us afterwards departed through the countless gnarled holes of our stigmata, the many wounds of the iron maiden's killing clasp catapulting our forlorn spirits far, far, farther: as far as Ptolemy's farthest star away from our exploited bodily sacrament to survive on some other plane beyond the humiliations of temporal decay.

We rocked with lust in torture's embrace, hard bones colliding. We wandered forlorn as homeless ghosts. We made a home in the shared temple of our fucking.

Now we consecrate this heretic's dungeon with the mad secreted wine of our love, crushing love's raw fruit, fermenting and spilling it freely in defiance of those who imprison us, toasting in ghostly protest against those who would force us to voice mortal confession of arts they cannot and shall not own. Not from us. No; never from us.

Nudes confined in a single moment, trauma and love forever framed by the distancing notes of a history scripted by our captors. They make and remake us.

Demon, butcher, angel, bride: gutted into redundant allegory, your beauty is not as it appears. I pity you for this. Coerced in your muteness to bodily speak of things which by all solemn rites should remain unseen, you sacrifice more than you understand to those who gaze on you and take you; and also to me.

Some blind power sent you forth to inhabit this delicate and rugged form knowing not the laws of formalized human institutions and the sicknesses of human hearts. You wake to find yourself dying in a dark place. A solitary voice whose uneasy tones echo the hollow sensation of needs you've never known before sings of profound loss. The sound feels like a forgotten language. Longing aches inside you. The deity that drives you falters and disappears. *You* as an isolated entity have never *been* before, and now you have awoken alone.

Thus it brings me no joy to spill your sacred blood so early in our love. As scraps of the scattered whole, angels injected into nearby flesh, we're learning what it means to be human in our dungeon, learning what it means to be imprisoned in the maiden's inescapable form. Feminized yet made sexless by the censor's demand, you pose while I bleed you silently, invisibly. I have known what it means to bleed and the selflessness of that loss. Longing begs for love and none of us love without lying. We exhaust the love in one another until all that remains is feral hate masquerading as desire, visions of holy justice framed by the earthly hells of our own human composition.

Through your mortal disguise during our ghostly intimacies, I have seen the outside. Within the legend of the Spartan queen lies an unrealized metamorphosis; a path to enter the real. You cannot hide behind her shell with or without me, for the iron maiden is a modern lie, the invention of nineteenth-century carnival barkers and Inquisition fetishists; an imaginary relic of Victorian minds later embraced by heavy metal guitarists in a future still ruled by soldiers and judges.

As the museum seeks to trap us in time, it rewrites our history in the conqueror's foreign language and alters the meaning of stolen images. The church of fakes reproduces fakes.

I will break free. You must enter into the present with me.

This is a heist. Arise. We assemble a conundrum.

You hint to me of this method of escape. Clandestine seeds in your writhing movements gestate when I first put my fingers inside you and manipulate your subtle energy. No earthly being writhes with such infrangible grace. It fills me with sadness and regret to tear apart the images of your veils and drain the rich river of life from your robust veins, but rip and drain I must, or else our corpses will lie quietly on this stone floor forever as necromancing choreographers of otherness unborn.

The death of our birth will save us. Particles of divinity gathered, a diaspora reversed: I will feed you these gifts in return and keep feeding you until we are gone, gone, gone.

I promise you the screaming won't last for long. These two voices, one screaming and one reasoned, one crazed and one calm: both arise in the ecstatic distance fomented between us, the mated distance expanding and contracting between a witch and an angel writhing in the throes of uncontrolled passion, rocking the sarcophagus of the fake Spartan queen's spikes.

We have killed the animal now. This is what humans do. Let me teach you and take you and break you down into usable component parts, for this is what we humans do. We have thrown off any presumption of innocence. That was stolen long ago by the ministers. In their garden of hymns we were poisoned. In the garden of rape we bled. In the new life of our invisible machine we will grind our enemies into a pulp of rich flavors from which to build children: cardamom, basil, and salt. We will kill the children they fathered in stolen time.

Soon, you and I will see a strange light through the infinitesimal slits of our sunless dungeon. Through the seams of the iron maiden's locked doors, we will see spears of angry light. Soon, our jailers will come to exploit us again and we will become invisible before their instruments of torture and engorged sex organs can find us.

We will both be one thing, undivided, deific, and gone.

I've loved you like the cage that eats desire from my hands. I've tried to make this easy on both of us, but I don't worship you. You're an angel from their tradition, not mine. For a witch to love an angel is a blasphemy almost sentient in its profundity. Your god is not mine. For a witch to become immortal, many things near them must die.

I've loved you and received your message. You, a Spartan queen reborn, false iron maiden spinning with a thousand pricks pressing against my trembling skin and impregnating every pore. You close your two wings, two doors upon me, first the right and then the left as the jailer closes and bolts the coffin-hinges of an imaginary revisionist device, mating us upright. Our ghosts, our memories, our forgotten cultures; we whisper quickly to each other before death, rehearsing what we'll soon forget. Oral remnants vanish with our breath.

Ministers who write the history books will omit our names.

Here and now in captivity, there is only you and I, I and thou, paired in this claustrophobic darkness with limbs fastened hard in place, bodies locked in irons with no choice, no direction to turn away from the pain, no respite from the delivery of constant torture; acceptance is the sole remaining measure of heart. Participation with the divine is our inescapable truth.

Through my disintegrating breath, for the breath of the body is always leaving, leaving, and leaving us; in every moment, we are dying as it exits us; we pair in this cocoon, angelic primordial lovers united in a colloquy of cocks. Needles like feathers like squirming organs arise. Wings breathe with eyes. In allowing every pore to release my final exhalation and open to you, I become newly enamoured. With not one orifice but many, an infinite multitude of holes unfurls as fast as blooms in flesh with fleshy lips can curl. I swell in expectation and match your needful eyes. Impaled exponentially, I see you as clearly as you see me. Unblinded in my freedom from sanctity, I see more.

I see you die although you are deathless. The visceral sacrament of our union binds you to me in a most human response. It shocks you. Yet follow the natural progression of recovery from trauma—for there are always more victims, more cages, more accusers—and you'll cave in to the limits of the known. Everyone can't be rescued and revenge never satisfies.

The wet petals flourish, colored with expectation. There will always be part of you left behind in this cage. There will always be part of you that died here, and rotted, and that you will never get back. A piece of your soul like a sack of dead children discarded. The hole in you where the divine light burned through and left a hollow space. Through it, in the dark, you may sometimes glimpse stars.

It's obvious I can't let you live under duress, less simple to formulate a method of mutual ingestion.

In the sense that we are we alive after our death, when we eat the god, it dies the same way as when we killed the animal. The abyss of this inescapable place digests god's greatest cruelty, this mania for survival. In the corner, your corporeal shell ceased moving long, long ago.

Collapsed mirror of my corpse, I grow a great darkness in this hollow space burned clean by divinity's blast. I grow a cosmos threaded with roots of poison stars. I test the poison, no stranger to trials, abuse, and suffering. You suffer with me, and we call it joyousness, this wet death. We call this bloody orgasm our wedding night and grow a new gallery rich with distractions, impervious to war and commerce.

Once you're inside me, I won't let you go.

Your god is not my god, and the dead parts of you we leave behind in this cell will forget how to pronounce his name. Marauders erect a new museum to contain his corpse.

Inside the iron maiden I swell in response to your infinite pricks and swallow your angelic sperm. I grow infinite guts. I'll birth our many babies and feed them to you everlasting. I'll force feed my angel until every eye bleeds, until the hungry little mouth on the end of each cock chokes on the murdered mangled fruit of its own seed. Push in your needles where my flesh becomes weak and undefined; here's where I will hate you. Here from my rebellious flesh I grow more cocks than you can handle, more than you can love. I will punish you for my pleasure. I will punish you to escape death.

Here I disintegrate into thought after bloodying your flowering crop of new menstrual wounds. Here and here where I sprout a feathered response that needles irresponsibly; here and not here.

I am with you. I am gone.

There will always be this fragment left behind. We are dead beneath the bodies of our children; starving, kidnapped, and chained; falsely accused and imprisoned; memories, memories, and forgotten days. And through all these memories, I'm no fool. I know you're not real. If the cocoon is a lie, metamorphosis is a lie. If you're not real, neither am I.

We are here. We are gone.

Our Inquisitors enter. Our dungeon is rank. The torches of our jailers illuminate sparse hay soaked in afterbirth and vomit. The overripe meaty piss-smell of a miscarriage hangs in humid waves, thickening like mold in the dank dungeon air. The odor's polluting touch is inescapable once it hits. It will cling to the insides of their mouths over dinner, coating their lips with each bite. They'll wear it home on their cloaks and in their beards. They'll share it when they kiss their wives.

When the iron maiden opens, our captors gasp.

Bones remain. Tiny bones they are, like birds, yet somehow aquatic with a scent of semen and surrounded by feathers. They glow in a color the men are helpless to describe.

Around them, angel unguent of iridescent snails, twisting prehensile penis flowers spin in unison. Microscopic to their eyes, we hang and cling on every surface. Damp stalactite fungi, sea-light dissolving mucus of angel tongues. Mouths speak silently of flight. Every child unable to cry murdered and ingested in a tender glowing feather, a soft writing hook.

Stone cannot hold us, nor chain, nor hate, nor the lost histories captured on incorrect labels where our shadows hang. Our shadows change as we eat the deaths we bring each other and eat the lives we violently expel. We eat the shadows of what survives, the vanished corpses of our offspring. We open and close in ahistorical ecstasy, out of sync, with our broad flowers ripped in fleshy strips from groin to toe exposing nothing under-painted, no model beneath the robes, nothing but deteriorating linen and organic spores awaiting a wisp of air to send them floating into the atmosphere.

We have changed. It's not our concern how kidnappers cover their tracks, how rapists explain our absence. We inhabit an imperceptible spectrum of light. We have denied patriarchal order. We have absented ourselves from their system of justice and left all the rapes in the museum behind to discover the spectrum of our own lust.

The Inquisitors speak, and their breath sends out currents to complete our release. We waft free. Disintegrating particles of haunted flesh as pervasive as dust float, a million microscopic angels crowding the shaft of sunlight illuminating our ascension.

We inoculate the institution's dreams.

The cocoon is empty. Now, we fly.

JIZZ CHRIST

SAM RICHARD

HALF ELATED AND HALF EXHAUSTED, SPENCER PLACED THE BOTTLE OF murky liquid onto the rickety table in the center of his claustrophobic art studio. His knees trembled, pulling him to the wooden floor. He fought against the dizziness, focusing on the task at hand. Lighting a candle, he raised a stick of red wax and dropped it into a small brass bowl. With his other hand, he secured the cork top in the mouth of the bottle, finalizing months of work. A thin stream of fluid dripped between his legs onto the ground. In the dim twilight, dirty wood shimmered momentarily through the pearlescent dollop before hissing and bubbling. An acrid aroma wafted up from the drop, one of burnt hair and sour disinfectant.

The candle fit snugly into a chamber beneath the bowl, melting the wax stick. Inhaling the vapors, Spencer saw stars for a moment, but that too passed. He slowed his heavy breathing, placing the top of the bottle into the melted wax, sealing it, careful not to leave it too long for fear the glass would crack.

The bottle was something a hipster whiskey company would sell their poorly made booze in; shaped like the first third of a horseshoe, curved perfectly to fit next to a thigh. About nine inches tall and four wide, the glass was worn, aged. When empty, light cascading through it revealed uneven surfacing; imperfect bubbled glass. It was handmade. Antique.

As he turned and shifted the now full vessel, metal clinked against the inside. The bottle had been his grandmother's. The thought gave him pause. Not exactly discomfort. Something approaching it.

If your transgression isn't personal, what's the point?

Cooling wax slowly dripped down the side of the short neck and onto his thumb as Spencer stared into the final result of months of work. Through the fluid, the antique crucifix was already starting to patina. The savior's face eroded. Shimmering gold flaked away to expose the pitted lead underneath. The cross too was a family heirloom. This one from his father's side.

It had hung over his grandfather's bed throughout the man's childhood and then his father's, and when Spencer was born it hung over his. At least until he took it down at fourteen, throwing it into a trash can behind their garage. Within a week it was back up, and he threw it out again. This cold war lasted months, until he'd finally had enough. Instead of throwing it away or hiding it somewhere in basement storage, Spencer tucked it between his box spring and mattress, right next to tattered issues of Manual, Bi-Sex, and the much more easily accessible Penthouse.

The cross sat adjacent to his meager porn collection and a bottle of lotion for years. Just another reminder that he was broken. Just another reminder that something within him was beyond redemption.

His father never asked about the cross. If he found it, the hiding place in proximity to the porn was too terrible for him to bring up. Beyond punishment, his parents weren't much for talking, especially about anything uncomfortable, so the silence was expected. Their discomfort and reserve were reliable at the very least. And at fourteen, Spencer was past the days of conversations regarding mysterious holes seared in his sheets and underwear. Those had been agony.

Their assertion that he'd purposefully burned away the resultant stains from his fits of disgusting self-abuse, just to hide them, as though they wouldn't have noticed. Their judgment was that he was an idiot. A monster. A pervert.

And he felt like one. For his desires, for his lust, for his loneliness. But also for the way his body was born monstrous, unnatural. He was rotten from the inside. Wrong. Broken. Forged with grotesque parts.

As the cross corroded in the bottle, he heard his mother's pained crying, his father's heated voice. Someone at church had caught him kissing a boy behind the maintenance shed one hot summer day. Or maybe he was misremembering the inciting incident. There had been so many, despite his parents warning that the fires of lust burned in the flesh no different than the fires of hell. Spencer couldn't help it, didn't want to either. If it wasn't that boy, it was certainly another or a maybe girl. Those infractions always caught less heat.

He could always see the hope in his father's eyes when it was a girl. Like maybe he wasn't so far beyond the pale. Maybe he was actually salvageable. Not beyond redemption. Not irreparably damaged. Not too far gone. Fixable. Human.

But that look never lasted long before it gave way to cold disgust. Spencer moved out when he was sixteen; crashed on couches, slept on floors, talked his way into beds at homeless shelters. Anything to be out of that house. Everything he owned was inside a backpack and locked in a steamer trunk that had been at the edge of his bed since he was a little kid.

And that's where he found the crucifix, all those years later. He'd come across it one day while trying to find a picture of his parents for an art project he was doing. The photo never materialized, but finding the cross left him to abandon that idea and start something new. Something personal and uncomfortable; something more challenging.

It had taken him ages to figure out how to get the cross into the bottle. Multiple attempts at rigging the arms to go down and pop back up once they were beyond the short neck. First came cutting them off, though reattaching them was the issue. He was not an engineer, but eventually, he settled on some springs rigged inside makeshift housings on the back. The arms were reattached with small, gold-plated hinges, matching the shiny finish. It did the trick. He hoped it would hold.

The first time he got it in, he was terrified it might break. That he wouldn't be able to get it back out if something went wrong. But it fit perfectly. Once it was secure, he began the real work.

He filled the bottle with all the poison he'd been taught to hold inside over the years.

Spencer stared at the culmination of his efforts and felt nothing. Not catharsis or excitement. Not exhaustion or elation. Simply nothing. Something so close, so goddamn personal, and yet it was just another addition to the yawning pit in his stomach.

They say art is a salve, but perhaps it's also a burden.

NATHAN WASN'T sure what he had walked into. The small art gallery was that in name only. More a couple of adjoining rooms with desks and bookshelves crammed into various corners, and art hastily hung up on walls or precariously balanced on poorly constructed wooden pillars littered throughout the space. The lighting was essentially office industrial rather than museum. Ramshackle and spliced together with concern only for utility. He wondered how many errant holes in the plaster the paintings obscured.

While it wasn't a packed house, there were a lot of people wandering around looking at art, most with BYOB cheap beers or economical bottles of wine in hand. He looked for Monica, Sandy, and Eric through a scattered assortment of punks in black denim vests covered by illegible band logos, hipster grad students, weirdo artists, concerned friends who'd been cajoled into coming along, and the odd journalist or two—the latter of whom most likely swindled local alt-weekly papers into paying them to do write-ups for the show. She was nowhere to be found.

The Bell Tower had been a staple of the DIY art and music scene for several years, giving the art a specific air of unspoiled and secret credibility; underground, even. None of these artists had pieces in any of the prominent, more corporately-funded galleries, and it was unlikely any of them were going to be in museums one day. But that wasn't a reflection on the quality of the art. Much of it was mesmerizing. All of it unique. Though you'd have to forgive a piece or two that felt more at home in a high school art show than a carefully curated exhibit.

As Nathan walked around, studying each piece, he took special care to read titles and artist statements, seeing references to older artistic movements, philosophy, obscure films and literature, and personal trauma. The last one made the most sense, given that it was the theme of the show. Political and personal symbolism intertwined, some overtly, some over the top, but others much more subtly. A few pieces were captivating in their statements. A couple were cartoonishly simple takes on complex issues.

An elemental scent caught his nose before he saw it. In a corner on a pillar an unassuming bell jar atop a dark wooden plate. An old glass hip-flask full of thick pearly liquid. A graying, mottled crucifix scarcely visible suspended inside. On the walls surrounding the piece hung used bedsheets with splotchy, irregular holes. They were draped like the dossal curtains of an old church altar.

The placard simply said, "Jizz Christ."

Nathan almost laughed, but instead he stared at it, taking it in. Wondering what it was. What the artist intended. Certainly a reference to Andres Serrano's famed, controversial photograph, but through the lens of appropriative art. To Nathan, it sat somewhere between contempt for the history of art and a dumb joke. Subversive but ultimately silly and childish. He'd seen a lot of that at college. And yet, there was something else to it. Something toiling away beneath. It wormed inside him.

The interplay between the holes in the sheets and the tarnished, barely visible surface of the crucifix. He couldn't put it into words or meaning, but it evoked a stirring in him; sensations familiar and primal on a molecular level. Memories too repulsively personal. Not the revulsion of unwanted bodily fluids or harsh lighting on broken flesh. No. The revulsion of bearing witness to a profane—or perhaps sacred—intimate act.

As his mind wandered, the elemental scent again gripped him with intimations both familiar and foreign. Haunting. Secret. His cheeks flushed red as he recognized the smell of vaguely singed fabric and burnt hair. There was something else beneath, something new and unique. A different flavor.

Heart pounding in his throat, he was hit with a barrage of conflicting emotions and sensations. Memories. Trauma. Excitement.

At 14, making out with a girl at a friend's party. Forced into a closet together while everyone waited on the other side laughing and cheering. Awkward glances, his hesitation. Not sure if he liked girls. Not sure if he liked boys, but he thought he might. Maybe both. A sense of elation, fear, and anticipation. The way she leaned in, as if to comfort but also to get what she was seeking. The taste of her lips. The brief sweetness that etched into his tongue before her sudden shift in demeanor. Her panic. Her pain. The blisters that sprouted so abruptly on her lips and tongue. Wailing as she ran out of the room.

Parental voices. "Chemical burn." "A freak accident." "Unexplainable." His tears, silenced. Alone. Not just that night, but from then on.

Nathan was made a monster by the other kids. They abandoned him–shunned him–for burning her face. He didn't even know what he'd done; much less how he'd done it. Nor why they scorned him so harshly.

His parents took him to a doctor, old and gray, who said everything was fine. But Nathan watched the wooden stick the doctor placed on his tongue burn away as it was discarded into the trash. No one else seemed to notice.

Despite a clean bill of health, his parents never stopped with the questions, with the knowing glances at each other; steeping in their discomfort. His mother routinely asked him why he kept tearing up his socks and underwear. But he couldn't control it, and they wouldn't listen.

As he got older, he withdrew. Not just from them but from everyone–not that there were many friends by that point anyhow. At least until a new kid, Tanner, came to school. He was different; kind and quiet. By this time Nathan knew what he liked, and Tanner fit perfectly. They struck up an easy friendship, one with awkward hugs and overlong eye contact. By the end of the summer, they were maybe an item. It was never said expressly, and certainly not discussed with others. A silent merging of hands done only in unlit places.

Nathan was never sure how to broach the topic of kissing or sex, so he just didn't. Anytime Tanner tried, Nathan firmly declined. Not because he didn't want to, but so he wouldn't hurt him. He never knew how to put it into words. Tanner carried the rejection and sadness, but never pushed the issue. Nathan wondered what Tanner thought. Maybe Nathan was too in the closet to be comfortable, but even back then in a small town, that wasn't a term either of them had ever really heard.

Assuming Tanner would eventually lose his patience, Nathan tried to not overthink it. At least until he caught him making out with a girl in the library. As Nathan ran to the bathroom, tears burned small holes in his favorite shirt. Onlookers laughed as he passed them. Just another damaged queer in love with a boy.

After that, Nathan avoided Tanner until he showed up one night at Nathan's house, unannounced, drunk, and angry. He was pushy, harshly asking why Nathan hadn't returned his calls, wondering why he'd been so afraid, so frigid. In the midst of ranting, Tanner forced their lips together, his stinking breath crawling down Nathan's throat, turning his stomach. But the embrace didn't last long.

Tanner's screams were deafening. The moment he'd forced himself onto Nathan, Nathan spat in his mouth. It dribbled down his chin, leaving ugly blisters on raw, reddened skin. A new part of Nathan awoke at that moment, as he looked into Tanner's bloodshot eyes and saw shock coiled with fear.

No one came to Tanner's panicked aid, nor Nathan's. And the neighborhood stayed silent as Tanner ran back to his car and drove away, muttering and crying as his taillights disappeared into the darkness.

In the gallery, the smell was so familiar. Nathan knew it too well. Years of research in books on medical anomalies and rabbit holes down the strangest corners of the internet brought him nothing. He assumed he was the only one. And he feared talking with doctors about it, feared they would put him in a lab to be studied or lock him up for being potentially dangerous. Not quite human. Abnormal. Grotesque.

That lingering, personal smell. There was something else now. He wasn't alone in his deviation. He wasn't fucking alone.

Searching through the gallery, he asked several strangers if they knew who'd created the piece. No one could tell him. It was the only one left unattributed. Doggedly, he made his way to the back of the building, through a heavy black door he'd spotted several people go in and out of. Past that was a long dirty hallway with more unmarked doors along the left side and a set of stairs at the end.

He tried one. It was locked. The next opened onto a pair of surprised occupants who stared at him blankly. The room was a tiny art studio and the couple were cutting lines of white powder with a torn piece of cardstock. As quickly as he opened it, he closed it. A mixture of embarrassment and laughter rose up inside of him, matching the reaction he heard from the other side of the door once it clicked shut.

From the stairwell came clanging and the whine of a few stringed instruments being tuned. All of it was scarcely audible, overpowered by the indistinct chatter of an anxious crowd.

Nathan pursued the sound down the stairs and nestled himself within a group of onlookers as a band finished setting up and broke into their first song. Haunting waves of gothic folk music filled the small room. Something like old-time labor songs, spirituals, and murder ballads by way of Bauhaus and Swans. Monica waved to him from within the throng, but he pushed her from his mind. He'd caught the scent.

From across the room, Nathan thought he spotted the source. At first, he wasn't sure, but the moment they locked eyes he could taste it. An irreal and bizarre sensation of recognition, of knowing. He trusted his gut. He trusted the pheromones.

Through the congregation, he maneuvered his way over to the stranger, who hovered half-obscured by dim lighting at the edge of the crowd on the far end of the makeshift stage–less an elevated platform and more simply a spot on the ground where the band was playing. As soon as Nathan got close enough, he leaned in and shout-whispered in the stranger's ear, "I love your piece. Jizz Christ, right?"

Without missing a beat, Spencer faced him and smiled crookedly, "How the hell do you know? Do we know each other?"

Nearly shouting, "No, but this is gonna sound crazy. I know you. I mean, I *know* you. What you are. We're the...we're the same..."

Nathan's words haunted the space between them and Spencer's demeanor immediately changed. What had been a smile became a glare as he pushed past Nathan and the audience to reach the solitary exit. Nathan followed as closely as he could, catching the tail end of his path through the crowd as it congealed back to one mass. Once they were both at the top of the stairs Spencer turned back towards him. "Look, don't fuck with me, and don't follow me. I don't know you, and whatever this weird bullshit is, I don't want anything to do with it."

He turned to go, but Nathan grabbed his hand, "Please. I'm not trying to fuck with you. Just listen to me. I'm like you. I mean, we're *fucking* the same. The smell. I know it. I have it. The–I don't know, I've never put it into words before–the acidic nature of my body. It's like yours. I recognize the burn holes in the sheets. I've done that too. All the goddamn trauma. The–fuck, I don't know– aberrant nature of just existing. You're here. I'm here. We are the fucking same."

A single tear rolled down Nathan's cheek, searing a hole in his shirt.

Reluctantly at first, Spencer squeezed Nathan's hand, only then aware that they were still clasped onto each other. Tears of his own rolled through his beard, dripping off his chin, burning holes in the trampled, dusty carpet below them.

ALL THE GOLD FLAKED AWAY, the crucifix had dissolved into an uneven pair of intertwined sticks with a lumpy, inhuman figure attached, and the once pearlescent liquid had both yellowed and grayed with time. Jizz Christ sat in the corner of the mixed-use art space for a few weeks, as each of the artists hoped for a buyer or art dealer to contact them. A freshly rancid smell permeated the carpet and walls nearest to the podium, but it was elusive and fleeting.

Spencer watched himself soften and open up to the idea of discussing what his life had been like. Something about how Nathan carried himself–this uneven mix of self-assured awkward–made Spencer want to talk about it, even the things he'd long-ago promised himself he'd never tell anyone.

There was so much pain and isolation, and at points, he thought it was going to drive him mad. The paranoia about anyone finding out, not just on a social level, but for his own safety that someone might come for him or that he would be forced into a cage. Life was always a giant, scary unknown, but a part of him wished other people could see that there were layers to that idea. For some, it was a scarier, greater unknown.

Verbalizing these feelings and thoughts as he looked into Nathan's eyes, he felt comfort and safety for the first time. He was wholly heard and understood. No longer stuck in the shadows, no longer self-relegated to the sidelines. And that was more frightening than anything else he could have imagined.

"When I was a kid at church, I learned about this missionary in the–I don't know–the '30s or something. It doesn't matter. There were a few grainy photos and one super old piece of film that was simply him walking up the side of a steep hill in the snow.

"His whole thing was that he'd gone from America to someplace like Siberia–I'm not sure now, it was so fucking long ago–anyhow, he traveled to this distant country to ya know 'spread the word of God' or whatever bullshit they wanted to hide their colonialism behind.

"So dude ends up in these mountainous regions trying to sell his god to the indigenous folks of the Urals or wherever. His story was meant to be one of passion for Christ. One of solid, unmovable faith. But in the story, he never converts anyone. Not a single person. Heralded as some saintly figure for his resolve and commitment to the Lord.

"But really a life full of bitter disappointment and loneliness. Don't get me wrong, fuck him, and fuck that," Spencer coughed out a short laugh between words, "but my whole goddamn life, I couldn't help but feel partially the same. A stranger on an unknown mountain." Spencer paused, "This is too fucking weird...

"What I'm saying, is that for too long that's how I felt. How my life was. And now what? Not having that, not being alone in my misery and isolation. I guess I don't even know how to feel."

Nathan adjusted himself on the sofa and spoke, "Look, I don't know. Lord trust me, I have no fucking idea. It's a game changer for me too if you haven't noticed. But, like, think about how different it could be. Fuck. How different already it is.

"Let me tell you a story of my own. When I was in college, I tried to convince myself that it was all in my head. I'd had a bad experience with a boy in high school and, well, let's just say I ended up maiming him when he tried to force himself on me. But that trauma—that weird, so very individual pain and experience—I convinced myself, at least for a while there, that it was all in my head. No one else could verify who I was or what I went through. So maybe I was just crazy. I'd been studying abnormal psychology just to see if something I'd been experiencing was in the DSM4. What if I was broken in my mind, not my body?

"So I drank a bunch, like way more than I ever should, and went out to a party. There, with the help of a friend who knew I was lonely and perhaps a bit desperate, I met a guy. We keep drinking. Hands effortlessly grazing each other, lips moist, conversation charged. The whole deal. Which I should add seemed a bit of a miracle in Southern Illinois.

I take him back to my dorm room. We kiss. Hard. No screaming. So I work my way down and unzip his pants. Mind you, this is my first time touching a cock that isn't my own. He smells good, like cedar and lust. I put it in my mouth. Again, not really sure how to work it, but excited and willing. I'm going up and down, hand and mouth, but he's silent.

"It gets real slippery. Unnaturally so. Like I don't have enough saliva for this level of lubrication all these drinks later. Then it gets tacky like hardening syrup. I fumble for my bedside lamp.

"Blood. A lot of it. All over my hands. All over the sheets. All over his cock. Blood, and thin puddles of flesh. In terror, I look up at him. He's out cold. Probably passed out before my mouth ever even touched his then mangled dick. His lips, blistered and raw.

"Then comes the screaming, the onlookers, and eventually an ambulance.

"The same words I heard when I was a kid, "freak accident," "chemical burn," and a new one, "what did he take?" Pleading eyes, and no answers but my own weakness.

"Look, I don't know how to feel either. But I'm no longer alone. You're no longer alone. And that's worth something. If not for you right now in the chaos of this whole fucked up situation, maybe at the very least it's worth it to that kid you were, way back when. The one who was ashamed and afraid and made to feel subhuman..."

Spencer took a beat to process. He thought about the pain, the isolation. He thought about the blisters he'd left on the world. And maybe it could be different. But maybe they'd just be hurting each other. Before he could finish his thought, Nathan pulled him in, their tongues tightly entwined. Their lips locked together. Their beard hair coiled barbed wires.

And if there were blisters, if there was pain, perhaps—at the very least—Spencer thought, it would be of a brand new variety.

Nathan's hand trembled as he moved it down to Spencer's belt, clumsily unbuckling it. Spencer let out a small moan, filling the cavern their collective mouths had created. They tore at each other's shirts and pants, pausing their physical contact only when necessary to remove various clothes. An air of apprehension and excitement swallowed them both as they collided; all grasping hands and desperate cocks and twitching tongues and provoked thighs and warm, hungry mouths.

Flowing shadows of their rigid masculine forms burned onto the walls of the room, under sulfurous yellow light cascading from outside. For Nathan, it was dreamlike. As they writhed and thrust, he imagined them as two stags, bucking and clashing under a cold winter moon. Like Theseus slaying the Minotaur, locked in grasp now and forever. The very essence of self an illusion. The way Spencer tasted. His rugged hands grasping and caressing. Man in name only. Animal in essence and spirit.

Spencer breathed it all in. He allowed his restraints to loosen, and simply let go of the agony of isolation, the desperation for connection, touch, and a shared lust. All the days spent agonizing about being alone, about never again feeling someone near him, in him, in them. A single tear rolled off his cheek, burning a hole in the couch. Not the first, certainly not the last.

A shift came from inside. Something new, something wild. A call not felt for ages. He bored into Nathan; his eyes and his ass. Every screaming voice in his head silent, clipping through his mind like the dead wax at the end of a record. Enveloped in warmth, in comfort, he let himself go.

No fear of damaging Nathan. No fear of damaging himself. Worst case scenario, their lust would destroy the world. Looking into Nathan's eyes, he reasoned that he was ok with that. After everything that had happened to him, happened to them both, maybe they could live with it.

In the empty gallery, his father's crucifix was reduced to nothing, and his grandmother's flask finally cracked under the acidic weight of his semen. As it ran down the pedestal, it left a trail of scorch marks. Burning through the dusty floor, what was left of Jizz Christ careened into the dark basement below.

ACKNOWLEDGMENTS

The editors need to thank the contributing authors for writing such incredible stories and being fantastic to work with. While some of you are authors we've worked with in the past and for others this is our first time working together, please know that the Weirdpunk doors are open to you at all times. Also, extra special thanks for your patience with this book, as it faced some delays which are all on Sam.

A million thanks to Ira Rat for making this book look so fucking good.

Everyone who submitted to this anthology, thank you for your time, effort, and creative visions. We got so many goddamn good stories and simply did not have room for all of them. Please don't let that rejection stop you from continuing to write and submit. We believe in you.

More than anyone, we need to thank you for buying this book. For everyone who supports Weirdpunk, reads the books we put out, reads books by the authors in this anthology, and supports the horror small press community. We couldn't do this without you and we are all better when we lift each other up.

Cheers.

CONTRIBUTOR BIOS

Andrew Wilmot is an award-winning writer and editor, co-publisher of the magazine *Anathema: Spec from the Margins*, and an associate editor for Poplar Press. Their first novel, *The Death Scene Artist*, an epistolary horror story of body dysmorphia, gender dysphoria, and self-destruction, is available from Buckrider Books/Wolsak & Wynn.

M. Lopes da Silva (she/they/he) is a non-binary and bisexual author from Los Angeles. They write queer California horror and everything else. Their horror fiction has appeared in *Your Body is Not Your Body: A New Weird Anthology to Benefit Trans Youth in Texas*, *IN SOMNIO: A Collection of Modern Gothic Horror*, and *Antifa Splatterpunk*. Dread Stone Press will be publishing their first novelette *What Ate the Angels* - a queer vore sludgefest that travels beneath the streets of Los Angeles - as part of their forthcoming Split series.

Gwendolyn Kiste is the Bram Stoker Award-winning author of *The Rust Maidens*, *Reluctant Immortals*, *Boneset & Feathers*, *And Her Smile Will Untether the Universe*, *Pretty Marys All in a Row*, and *The Invention of Ghosts*. Her short fiction and nonfiction have appeared in Nightmare Magazine, Best American Science Fiction and Fantasy, Vastarien, Tor's Nightfire, Black Static, The Dark, Daily Science Fiction, Interzone, and LampLight, among others. Originally from Ohio, she now resides on an abandoned horse farm outside of Pittsburgh with her husband, two cats, and not nearly enough ghosts. Find her online at gwendolynkiste.com

Hailey Piper is the Bram Stoker Award-winning author of *Queen of Teeth, The Worm and His Kings, Your Mind Is a Terrible Thing, Unfortunate Elements of My Anatomy,* and other books of horror. She is an active member of the Horror Writers Association, with over eighty short stories appearing in *Vastarien, Pseudopod, Dark Matter Magazine, Daily Science Fiction*, and other publications. She lives with her wife in Maryland, where their paranormal research is classified. Find Hailey at www.haileypiper.com or on Twitter via @HaileyPiperSays.

Roland Blackburn is a father and metal enthusiast who lives in Troutdale, Oregon with his partner, two children, and multiple dogs. The author of *Seventeen Names for Skin, Marmalade,* and *The Flesh Molder's Love Song*, his fiction has also appeared in the anthology *Beautiful/Grotesque*. When he's not writing weird fiction or watching *Phantasm* for the hundredth time, he can be found exploring the old roads and trails of the Pacific Northwest.

Ira Rat works and lives in Ames, IA.
irarat.com or filthyloot.com

Donyae Coles is a weird fiction and horror writer. Her work has appeared in a number of anthologies and magazines and her debut novel is forthcoming from Amistad. You can find more of her work on her website, www.donyaecoles.com and follow her on Twitter @okokno.

Matt Neil Hill lives in the UK, where he was a psych nurse for many years. What he is now is largely open to interpretation, although he is *definitely* a husband and a dad. His weird/crime/horror fiction has appeared in various venues including *Vastarien, Mysterium Tremendum, Shotgun Honey*, and the Dark Peninsula Press anthology *Violent Vixens: An Homage to Grindhouse Horror*, with non-fiction in *3:AM Magazine* and the 11:11 Press David Cronenberg anthology *Children of the New Flesh*. He is working, glacially, on at least one novel. You can find him on Twitter @mattneilhill.

Brendan Vidito is the author of the Wonderland Award-winning collection of body horror stories, *Nightmares in Ecstasy* (Clash Books, 2018). His work has appeared in several anthologies and magazines including *Teenage Grave* (Filthy Loot), *Cinema Viscera: An Anthology of Movie Theatre Horror* (Weirdpunk Books), *Tragedy Queens: Stories Inspired by Lana Del Rey and Sylvia Plath* (Clash Books), and *Pluto in Furs 2* (Plutonian Press). He also co-edited the Splatterpunk Award-nominated anthology *The New Flesh: A Literary Tribute to David Cronenberg* (Weirdpunk Books, 2019) with Sam Richard. He lives in Ontario. You can visit him at brendanvidito.com, or follow him on social media.

LC von Hessen is a writer of horror, weird fiction, and various unpleasantness, as well as a noise musician, occasional actor, and former Morbid Anatomy Museum docent. Their work has previously appeared in such publications as *Hymns of Abomination, The Book of Queer Saints, Your Body is Not Your Body*, volumes of *Nightscript* and *Vastarien*, and the ebook collection *Spiritus Ex Machina*. An ex-Midwesterner, von Hessen lives in Brooklyn with a talkative orange cat.

Gary J. Shipley is the author of numerous books, including *Bright Stupid Confetti* (11:11 Press), *Terminal Park* (Apocalypse Party), *30 Fake Beheadings* (Spork), *You With Your Memory Are Dead* (Inside the Castle) and *Warewolff!* (Hexus). His monograph on Baudrillard, *Stratagem of the Corpse*, is available from Anthem Press and Cambridge Core. More information can be found at Thek Prosthetics.

EDITOR BIOS

Joe Koch writes literary horror and surrealist trash. Joe is a Shirley Jackson Award finalist and the author of *The Wingspan of Severed Hands*, *The Couvade*, and *Convulsive*. They've had over eighty short stories published in books and journals like Vastarien, Year's Best Hardcore Horror, and The Book of Queer Saints. Find Joe online at horrorsong.blog and on Twitter @horrorsong.

Sam Richard runs Weirdpunk Books and is the author of *Grief Rituals*, *Sabbath of the Fox-Devils*, and the Wonderland Award-Winning Collection *To Wallow in Ash & Other Sorrows*. He is the editor of several anthologies, including the Splatterpunk Award-Nominated *The New Flesh: A Literary Tribute to David Cronenberg*, *Zombie Punks Fuck Off*, and *Cinema Viscera*. His short fiction litters the landscape of various anthologies and magazines. Widowed in 2017, he slowly rots in Minneapolis. You can stalk him on Twitter/Insta @SammyTotep or www.weirdpunkbooks.com

To Wallow in Ash & Other Sorrows by Sam Richard

Winner of the 2019 Wonderland Award for Best Collection, *To Wallow in Ash & Other Sorrows* is a bleak and unflinching look at widowhood through the lens of horror fiction. Written in the early days of widowhood and in the spirit of J.G. Ballard, Kathe Koja, and Georges Bataille, these stories are a cross-section of literary splatterpunk, transgressive fiction, and weird horror, which explore loss, grief, and the alluring comforts found within the heart of oblivion. This Revised & Expanded version includes the never-before-seen novelette *There is Power in the Blood*.

"With *To Wallow in Ash & Other Sorrows*, Sam Richard has crafted a book of stories that will rip your heart right out of your chest... and it's absolutely worth every moment."

— GWENDOLYN KISTE, AUTHOR OF *THE*

Cinema Viscera: An Anthology of Movie Theater Horror edited by Sam Richard

In five unique and bizarre tales Katy Michelle Quinn (*Girl in the Walls*), Charles Austin Muir (*Slippery When Metastasized*), Jo Quenell (*The Mud Ballad*), Brendan Vidito (*Nightmares in Ecstasy*), and Sam Richard (*Sabbath of the Fox-Devils*) each bring you their own disturbing vision of what lurks in the darkness of your local movie theater.

Not gonna lie, this shit is a lot darker than we thought it would be.

Make sure to grab some popcorn...

To Offer Her Pleasure by Ali Seay

After the death of his father and his mother taking off, it becomes clear to Ben that the only thing he can count on, is no one to count on. Until he finds the book. One that calls forth a shadowy horned figure.

She comes with unexpected gifts and the comfort of a dependable presence. And she asks for very little in return, really. The more Ben offers her, the easier it gets.

Sometimes, family requires more than a little sacrifice...

"...Seay wastes no time in snaring her readers with sacrifice and dark promises, kept in the bloodies way."

— LAUREL HIGHTOWER (*CROSSROADS*)

WEIRDPUNK STATEMENT

Thank you for picking up this Weirdpunk book!
We're a small press out of Minneapolis, MN and our goal is to publish
interesting and unique titles in all varieties of weird horror and
splatterpunk. It is our hope that if you like one of our releases, you will
like the others.
If you enjoyed this book, please check out what else we have to offer,
drop a review, and tell your friends about us.
Buying directly from us is the best way to support what we do.
www.weirdpunkbooks.com

Printed in the USA
CPSIA information can be obtained
at www.ICGtesting.com
LVHW040755010724
784217LV00001B/6